BLACK LIMERICKS

Ranjit Lal was born in Kolkata in 1955, and educated in Mumbai, graduating in Economics and Sociology. As a freelance writer and columnist, he has over a thousand articles, short stories, features, and photo-features published in over fifty newspapers and magazines in India and abroad. He has special interest in areas like natural history, photography, humour, satire and automobiles, on which he writes for both adults and children. He is one of the few Indian journalists to write satire and humour on a sustained basis.

He has authored several books including *The Simians of South Block and the Yumyum Piglets*; *The Crow Chronicles; The Life and Times of Altu Faltu; That Summer at Kalagarh; The Bossman Adventures; Enjoying Birds; Birds of Delhi; Birds from My Window; The Caterpillar Who Went on a Diet and Other Stories; When Banshee Kissed Bimbo,* and *The Battle for No. 19*. Ranjit Lal lives in Delhi.

BOOKS BY THE SAME AUTHOR

The Life & Times of Altu-Faltu
The Small Tigers of Shergarh
The Simians of South Block and the Yumyum Piglets

OTHER INDIAINK TITLES

Anjana Basu	*Black Tongue*
Anjana Basu	*Chinku and the Wolfboy*
Anjum Hasan	*Neti, Neti*
A.N.D. Haksar	*Madhav & Kama: A Love Story from Ancient India*
Boman Desai	*Servant, Master, Mistress*
Chitra Banerjee Divakaruni	*Shadowland*
Haider Warraich	*Auras of the Jinn*
I. Allan Sealy	*The Everest Hotel*
I. Allan Sealy	*Trotternama*
Indrajit Hazra	*The Garden of Earthly Delights*
Jaspreet Singh	*17 Tomatoes: Tales from Kashmir*
Jawahara Saidullah	*The Burden of Foreknowledge*
John MacLithon	*Hindutva, Sex & Adventure*
Kalpana Swaminathan	*The Page 3 Murders*
Kalpana Swaminathan	*The Gardener's Song*
Kamalini Sengupta	*The Top of the Raintree*
Madhavan Kutty	*The Village Before Time*
Pankaj Mishra	*The Romantics*
Paro Anand	*Pure Sequence*
Paro Anand	*Wingless*
Paro Anand	*Weed*
Paro Anand	*No Guns at My Son's Funeral*
Raza Mir & Ali Husain Mir	*Anthems of Resistance: A Celebration of Progressive Urdu Poetry*
Rakesh Satyal	*Blue Boy*
Sanjay Bahadur	*The Sound of Water*
Shandana Minhas	*Tunnel Vision*
Selina Sen	*A Mirror Greens in Spring*
Sharmistha Mohanty	*New Life*
Shree Ghatage	*Brahma's Dream*
Sudhir Thapliyal	*Crossing the Road*
Susan Visvanathan	*Something Barely Remembered*
Susan Visvanathan	*The Visiting Moon*
Susan Visvanathan	*The Seine at Noon*
Tushar Raheja	*Run Romi Run*

FORTHCOMING TITLES

Tanushree Podder	*Escape from Harem*
Rani Dharker	*Anurima*

BLACK LIMERICKS

RANJIT LAL

First published in 2011
IndiaInk
An imprint of
Roli Books Pvt Ltd
M-75, Greater Kailash II Market
New Delhi 110 048
Phone: ++91 (011) 4068 2000
Fax: ++91 (011) 2921 7185
E-mail: info@rolibooks.com; Website: rolibooks.com

Also at
Bangalore, Chennai, Jaipur, Kolkata, & Mumbai

Cover design: C'Sam Asung Muivah

ISBN: 978-81-86939-60-4

Typeset in Times New Roman by Roli Books Pvt. Ltd
and printed at Rakmo Press, New Delhi

1

'Mayyaaaa! Can't you hear the phone? Pick it up!'

Poor Bob Marley and The Wailers didn't stand a chance. Maya rolled her eyes and grimaced. Really she ought to have had the volume higher. Her mother's elephant-like trumpet had blasted clear through her bedroom door, though admittedly, she had heard the phone (warbling weakly in comparison) too and hoped someone else would pick it up.

'Mayaaaa! I said pick up the phone!'

'God what a voice!' Maya muttered, swinging her long legs off the bed, 'she could bring down chandeliers with it!' A quirky grin broke through and her lips began twitching as the limerick presented itself, readymade as always.

My mom has a voice like a drill
So shrill it can make you quite ill
If you pretend you can't hear
And say 'beg pardon my dear?'
She'll turn you into roadkill!

She snorted back a giggle, and pushed back her lanky (mousy, she once heard someone remark) dark brown hair and lunged for the phone in the small hallway just outside her room.

'Hello?' she said, brushing her hair out of her eyes and smoothening her T-shirt down.

'Hello? Maya is that you? God, you took an age to pick up the phone! It's me, Jayant from England!'

'Oh hi Jay!' But Maya's oval face, pleasant enough with its grave dark brown eyes and straight (too long her mother thought) nose, had closed down rather like the leaves of a mimosa.

From England, Jayant's voice came, creamy and slightly patronizing. And had he already started affecting that awful posh snobbish accent, she noticed. He'd only been in England for six months for God's sake, and was already talking – no elocuting – (another quirky grin) – like some little Lord Fauntlelory.

'Er… I have some good news actually, sis,' Jay went on, making it sound as if it were no big deal really. Just what did he mean by calling her 'sis' instead of didi? 'I just won the school open golf championships. Beat all the sixth formers. I managed to hit five birdies in a row. And I've topped my class in all subjects again!'

'That's great Jay!' How nice for you little bro. 'Ma and Papa will be thrilled!' She took a deep breath. 'It's only me you know, so you don't have to elocute!' she added with some asperity. He was only thirteen dammit and shoulder high, (but round-faced, chubby-cheeked and good looking) and she was seventeen, long-legged and walked like a heron (she thought).

'Mr Lambeth the headmaster says I'll get a full scholarship next year!'

'Great! Mama and Papa will be thrilled,' she repeated automatically.

'Where are they? Hey, have your holidays started? And you know what? I'm thinking of taking up running – like you!'

Again Maya took a deep breath, please, please Jay don't do that – leave that for me at least.

'Oh,' she said weakly. 'How nice!' And then let slip, 'you know I ran for the "Run for Health" half marathon today.'

'Did you win?'

Maya rolled her eyes. She and her big mouth! Why did she always get herself into such a mess? When would she learn?

'No,' she admitted and then, reddening blurted, 'actually I got lost! They hadn't marked the route properly!'

'What?' squeaked Jay incredulously. 'You got lost? How could you get lost while running with five-hundred people?'

'It's no big deal really; you know how I tune out when I run. I must have missed a turn or something. About halfway through I found myself running alone in this narrow stinking gully.'

'God, do you close your eyes and run?' Jay was exasperated – as one might be with a six year old who is still not toilet-trained. 'Why didn't you stick with your friends – or with a group?'

'Umm… Well I lost them too. There were so many people milling about at the start I got separated from them too.' She exhaled. 'And then the starter's pistol went off and there was total confusion. Actually what does it matter where you run as long as you're running.'

'God you're so vague, Maya. You'll never win anything with that attitude!'

Just can't you shut up and stop lecturing you little shrimp! 'Hell who wants to win anyway?' she countered.

But of course she did. Desperately. Anything.

'Next time you run do a recce of the course. And don't be so vague. You're so woolly headed.' And then, because he was insatiably curious, 'By the way what happened? How did you find your way back?'

'Well it was simple. There was this dead end so I just turned around and ran all the way back. Then one kind woman pointed out a shortcut and I took that and … and re-joined the race.'

'Did you at least finish?'

'Of course I did. What did you think?'

Actually she had dared not re-join the race for fear of finishing dead last amidst jeers and laughter. She had run blindly – and instinctively – all the way home even as a few puzzled passers-by had shouted that she was running the wrong way. Certainly she had loped a longer distance than the others. In future, she would do her running in private she decided, and not participate in these public tamashas. She loved running and reveled in the wonderful springy rhythm she developed, and the cool wash of wind against her hot cheeks, and the sheer sense of physical well-being as her strong legs loped effortlessly, stride after long stride. Most joggers looked tortured while running, Maya looked blissful, happily 'tuned out' as she had said. But now, another terrible limerick was forming, like some evil genie emerging from a lamp. What she had begun as exercise to distract herself from thoughts that upset her had turned around and bitten her as it were. Now her limericks were mostly directed stingingly at herself.

I lost my way in the race
And didn't dare show them my face
So I ran all the way home,
To sulk all alone
Why am I such a poor hopeless case?

She grimaced. It was godawful. And why did she so flog herself like this all the time? Masochistic bitch she was.

'Are you still making up those awful limericks?' Jayant asked, guessing uncannily what her sudden silence probably meant.

'Yes, and they're not silly. They're fun.'

'God sis, please spare me. Why don't you write something proper instead? Like poetry? Grow up!'

'Because I hate poetry!' She didn't of course, but now perforce had to. 'And don't sis me Jay, just because you're in Eng…'

From downstairs her mother trumpeted again like an irritated she elephant. 'Maayyyaaa! Who's on the phone? Will you stop talking! Put it down. You know Jay raja rings up at this time.'

Oh shit! She popped her head out of her room – where she had taken the phone – and called down.

'Ma, it is Jay!'

'What? You silly girl, why didn't you tell me? You've been talking nonsense for half and hour making him spend all that money! These international calls are so expensive. He must have finished all his pocket money poor boy. Jay raja – how are you beta?'

Quietly Maya put down the receiver but stayed in the hallway so that she could hear her mother talk (not that she had to strain her ears for that). Mrs Sabherwal was in full flow, like a river in spate, carrying everything before it.

'Yes, beta we will be getting the flat renovated before you come for your holidays – the company has employed professional interior decorators for the job. You know I can't be near the place while it is being painted because of all my allergies. Anyway Papa and myself will come and fetch you – Papa has got some meetings in England – and he's got a free ticket for me. Maya didi will spend the summer at Pankaj Mama's beach resort where we will all join her when we return with you. You know we stayed there for a short while last year, but now he's added a special family wing where we will stay. And when you come maybe you can coach her in mathematics and other subjects. You know she has not been allowed to sit for her Boards this year.'

Upstairs, Maya shrank back into her room, her face a dead mask, biting her lip. She knew she would have to repeat the year and that would mean losing all her friends and having to mix with the junior crowd, who would snigger and call her 'didi' or 'auntie', no doubt. She had tried to simply put it out of her mind as much as possible. Now she concentrated on the first part of the conversation she had overheard. So they were to go – she was to be sent to – Pankaj Mama's beach resort – Shanbagh Beach Resort – for the summer. Why was she always the last to be told about such things? Even now, her mother had not actually informed her – she had overheard it. But yes, she had told Jay raja – he was told everything. It was as if she just did not exist – or worse – as if her existence did not matter.

'As if I'm just this background person,' she gulped, surprised at how quickly the tears had brimmed over and the frog in her throat had started jumping. Of course there was no question of her being taken abroad – it was too expensive, like those international calls. A shriek from downstairs momentarily distracted her and she popped her head around her room door again.

'But beta how wonderful! A golf champion! Oh, Papa will be so proud. And first in class again! You should win that Roadside scholarship easily.'

Sure, Maya thought more bitterly than she wanted to. Jayant was definitely Rhodes scholar material. Tailor-made for it actually! Custom-made. But really why was she being such a bitch? No, think Shanbagh Resort. Where she would be spending the summer. They had spent a couple of nights there last year, on the way back from Goa. But now, from Delhi they would probably have to go to Mumbai first and drive from there for about four or five hours along the road to Goa. From here they would branch off westwards on a narrow bumpy road till they came to the sea. Her uncle had built a beautiful and very exclusive resort tucked away amidst casuarina plantations and coconut groves, which was chiefly frequented by rich (you had to be) foreigners. But by mid-May onwards, the lean season began as the summer really sizzled and the sea began to get a little rough anticipating the monsoon. And yes there was the beach and the sea. She could run to her heart's content with her eyes closed, yes she could. And then cool off blissfully in the sea – not actually swim in it of course because she was petrified of getting out of her depth – but just loll about in the shallows as cool lacy wavelets washed over her, looking up dreamily at the sky. No one would bother her. She thought about her cousins and screwed up her face. Hari (Harry he liked to be called, but really Harishchand – just what were his parents thinking!) was nineteen or maybe twenty, loud and overbearing, physically a bit of a buffalo really, and last year had tended to press too close against her for comfort. His hands had a disconcerting tendency to wander where they had no business to be. His sister Sherry (Sharmila really!) a year or so younger was devastatingly pretty and a complete airhead, harmlessly sweet. Well, she would ignore them to the extent possible – and suspected that she bored them anyway and that they called her 'bhenji' behind her back.

But at the moment Maya had a bone to pick with her mother. She came down the stairs as her mother put down the phone. Her mother looked up, a glow suffusing her chubby face, a tear glistening in her eye.

'Jay raja has won some big golf tournament, and he's come first in every paper!' she announced with a significant toss of her head and a mega-dose of innuendo.

'I know Ma he told me. So good for him! Ma, you never told me that we're going to Shanbagh this summer.' Almost an accusation.

'Actually you should be spending your holidays taking tuitions and not loafing on the beach,' her mother replied petulantly. 'But since the house has to be done up and Pankaj Mama has invited us we're going there. Papa will remain back here in Delhi and I will join him in Mumbai later, when we go to London to pick up Jay raja. You will remain at Shanbagh where we will return with Jay raja. Maybe he will be able to help you with your studies.'

Oh, and how great would that be! A tall lanky seventeen-year-old big sister, taking tuitions from her chubby faced thirteen-year-old little brother. How Hari and Sherry would smirk and snigger.

'When do we leave, ma?' she asked, as if she had a host of important appointments that had to be taken care of.

'We are flying to Mumbai on Thursday. Pankaj Mama is sending a car there and we should be at Shanbagh that evening itself.'

'For how long will we be there?'

'You'll be there for three weeks or a month at least. So you better pack a lot of clothes.'

But not her books! Maya shook her head firmly. No schoolbooks. No way she was going to be given lessons by chubby little Jay in his earnest posh voice. Not on your life.

'Okay ma,' she said. 'I might have to buy some T-shirts and shorts.'

'And think of some nice gifts for Sherry and Hari!' her mother ordered.

Maya screwed up her face. 'Ma they have everything. And anyway they give whatever we take for them to their servants.'

2

Mumbai airport was overcrowded and hot and Maya was glad when she hefted the last of their three suitcases off the conveyer belt on to their trolley. She put their hand baggage on top and manoeuvered it carefully through the crowd, frowning as she tried to control it. The damn thing appeared to have a mind of its own as it sidled this way and that. And then suddenly it sort of tripped over itself and tipped over, as a front wheel came off. Gleefully the three suitcases avalanched off it, catching a nattily suited and rather spherical Oriental gentleman bang on the kneecaps making him fall back on his (rather large) posterior with a thump and a gasp.

'Oh God, I'm so sorry! I hope you're not hurt!' Maya was mortified as she rushed forward to help the gentleman up.

'Mayaaa!' screeched her mother, so shrilly that all heads in the terminal turned in her direction, startled, 'Can't you even handle the trolley properly!'

The gentleman had recovered somewhat from the shock of finding himself on his bottom and glanced around bemusedly. Then he spotted the truant trolley wheel and realized what had happened. Maya, standing nearby opened and shut her mouth like a goldfish, repeating 'I'm so sorry! I'm so sorry!' The man nodded.

'It's okay, miss!' he grunted. 'Not your fault! These tlolleys are defective! I shall complain about them!'

'Thank you,' Maya stuttered and suddenly galvanized helped the gentleman to his feet. He dusted himself, adjusted his tie, smiled and waddled off, none the worse for his experience. Much relieved, Maya went off to fetch another trolley from the rank.

She was still red-faced when they wheeled their way out.

'Pankaj Mama said the driver would meet us here with a placard,' her mother said, as she surged out into the hall and looked around.

'There he is Ma,' Maya said, pointing to a smartly uniformed man holding up a placard that read, 'Mrs Sabherwal, Shanbagh Resort.' A sturdy looking boy with a shock of spiky black hair standing up vertically, stood next to him, perched on the railings and leaning over.

In no time, the chauffeur had moved forward smoothly and relieved Maya of the hateful trolley.

'Welcome to Mumbai, madam! Myself Srinivas,' he said, smiling. The boy, dressed in a rather smart striped black and dark blue T-shirt and black denim shorts, dropped down from the railing and dusted down his hands. He must be a little older than Jay, Maya guessed and like him was another half-pint-size, reaching up to her shoulders. He had a chubby somewhat baby face and a couple of front teeth peeped out, giving him a cute (Maya thought) rabbity look.

'Hi!' he said crisply, sticking out his hand, 'I'm Yash Ahuja, my parents are waiting in the lobby of the hotel nearby. We'll be travelling to the resort together.' He grinned at her and raised his caterpillar like eyebrows, as if to imply, 'like it or not!'

'Hi!' Maya said looking at his sparkling black eyes and shaking his proffered hand. 'I'm Maya Sabherwal and this is my mom!' She fixed her grave eyes on him, and went on, 'Nice to meet you Yash!' He seemed friendly enough, but she was wary, with boys this size you just never knew. Give them half a chance and they'd palm you a cockroach.

'Please wait here, madam,' Srinivas instructed. 'I'll just get the car.'

Five minutes later they were installed in the blue Qualis, which was already loaded up with luggage, and driving smoothly out.

'We pick up Mr and Mrs Ahuja from their hotel and drive straight to Shanbagh Resort,' Srinivas explained.

Mr Ahuja was a large, florid looking man, with a ruddy complexion and a rather loud voice. He had a warm, friendly smile though and was dressed in a beige safari suit and expensive brown loafers. His wife had too much rouge and blue stuff around her eyes (Maya thought) and jingled and tinkled with the large number of bracelets and trinkets she wore on her arms, ears and around her neck. She was about as tall as Maya and slim, dressed in canary yellow slacks and a floral top and had tied her hair in a loose, informal ponytail. But she had a warm, open smile too, which seemed infectious.

'Mom, Dad – this is Mrs Sabherwal and her daughter Maya,' said Yash making the introductions. 'Mrs Sabherwal, Maya – my mom and dad!' And Maya had to stifle a giggle half expecting the boy to bow. NRI, she thought accurately, pint-size is an NRI.

'I'm so glad to meet you, Maya,' Mrs Ahuja said. 'You must be looking forward to the beach. And Mrs Sabherwal, namasteji! So nice to meet you!'

'The kids can sit in the third row!' Mr Ahuja decided, as they settled into the car. 'Then everyone will be comfortable. Srinivas, how long will it take us to reach?'

'About five-six hours, sir,' replied Srinivas. 'We should be at the resort by five-thirty. The last part of the road is a little bumpy so it takes more time.'

Mrs Sabherwal, a naturally garrulous and friendly (if inquisitive) soul was soon deep in conversation with Mrs Ahuja (who was equally delighted to have company), and all too soon, telling her all about Jay and his accomplishments. Occasionally she would lower her voice though and Maya knew that she was now the subject of the conversation. At the back, Yash began playing some complicated looking beeping computer game, while Maya stared out at the passing scenery and tried not to think about what her mother was saying about her. She loved this road journey, especially after they had got onto the highway to Goa, which switchbacked through the Western Ghats. Occasionally she glanced at the sturdy fellow beside her and once he caught her glance and raised his caterpillar eyebrows interrogatively and grinned. She smiled back and raised her own (also rather shaggy, she thought) eyebrows and asked:

'What game is that? I'm quite hopeless at those you know! They give me panic attacks what with their beeps and sirens and flashing lights.'

'It's not a game,' he said deadpan serious. 'I'm writing a programme!'

'Ah,' she said, nodding knowingly, her eyes beginning to twinkle. 'Sure. With which, you will infect and destroy all the computers in the world I presume?'

'That too!' He stopped his game and leaned towards her.

'Say,' he whispered, all hush-hush, 'that was real cool!'

She frowned. 'What was cool?'

'The way you took out that geezer back there at the airport!'

'What geezer? I didn't take out any geezer anywhere!'

'Kneecapped him, I mean!'

'Oh that! I didn't kneecap him!' she replied indignantly. 'It was an accident!'

'Looked more like an IRA hit to me!' he said decisively. 'Straight wham into the kneecaps! Wish I could have done it!'

'Next time I get a trolley with a loose wheel I'll inform you!'

'Great!'

Her lips twitched again as the limerick arose wraithlike.

'Do you talk to yourself even in company?' Yash inquired, raising his caterpillar eyebrows heavenwards.

'I wasn't talking to myself!' Sheesh! He was a precocious kid!

'You were! I saw your lips moving!'

'I was only making up a limerick!'

'What? Limerick? Hah! You're having me on.'

'Listen, then….

A girl with a tellible tlolley
Lost a wheel that was loose and all wobbly
She kneecapped a large rotund shogun
Who toppled back on his bum-bum
But she escaped by saying I'm so solly!

His eyes widened incredulously, and then his face split open into a huge, huge grin of sheer delight.

'Wow! But that's great! Awesome! That's just so cool! Wow! I never heard anything like this before! You made that up just now? How do you do it?'

'It just pops into my head,' she said, blushing with pleasure. He was still shaking his head incredulously.

'I think it needs a bit of work on it though,' she added judiciously.

'I can't believe it!' Yash repeated, giving a sudden snort of laughter. 'A girl who produces limericks just like that! Pouf! Out of thin air!' And added wistfully, 'You're really lucky!' And maybe this great India experiment of his parents' wouldn't turn out so badly after all. If he could meet someone – even a girl – who could produce limericks out of thin air, within days of arriving, God knows what other happy surprises lay in store for him. Talk about the great Indian rope trick, man!

'Thanks,' she said, still blushing, a little embarrassed by her flushed cheeks and surprised by how pleased she felt. 'So where do you live Yash?'

He grimaced. 'Don't ask! Actually I don't even know! Been all over. My dad keeps getting transferred every six months. We were in Hong Kong last, but then they,' he jerked a finger towards his parents, 'finally decided I was going wild and losing out on India, so we've come back here to settle down.' He lowered his voice. 'Actually it was because I was expelled from all the schools in Hong Kong and they had nowhere to put me! I'm still wanted in Singapore! Can't ever go back there! They've scheduled me for execution in Changi prison.' He drew his forefinger across his throat and nodded slowly.

'What? Oh, I see! What did you do?'

He shrugged nonchalantly. 'Oh you know, the usual. Smoking, guns, drugs, booze, graffiti, vandalism, chewing gum, fast cars, chickies… stuff like that, the works really.'

'Hmm!' She nodded. 'Too bad.'

'At the last place they kicked me out for snogging the principal's daughter!'

'What? Snogging?'

'You know – kissing, smooching.' He grinned cheekily. 'Want a demo?'

'What? Don't you dare!' She was outraged, but could see his lips twitch. Aha – having her on was he… Again he shrugged. 'Sorry, no offence just thought you might like to know what snogging really is.' Very matter-of-fact like. He went on, 'Anyway, and then my parents found out that I had got dragons tattooed on my bum! They thought I'd joined a shogun outfit! They really freaked!'

'You have dragons tattooed on your bum? I don't believe you!'

'I could show you! Want to see?'

'Don't you dare! I don't want to see your butt!' She was appalled. It was time to cap the conversation and look out of the window again. She stole another glance at the cheeky fellow and saw his mouth twitch at the ends again. Aha!

They were passing through the Karnala Bird Sanctuary, and there in the distance, the Duke's Nose stood pointing skywards as it had done since time immemorial. Maya stared at it and swallowed the giggle that was bubbling up inside her. What a cheeky little rogue he was, but was he also trying to impress her?

'Are you okay back there?' Mrs Ahuja inquired as the car began looping along the ghat road. 'If you're feeling sick, I have some lemon drops you can suck!'

Yash rolled his eyes, made a retching noise and took a handful and went back to his computer game. Maya murmured a 'no thanks, I'm fine' and stared out of the window, thinking about Shanbagh and the beach.

At last they left National Highway 17 and struck off westwards and seawards. The road was narrower and decidedly more rutted as they came off the forested ghats, and now there was much less traffic. They passed through dim and deep mango and chickoo orchards (stopping to buy basketfuls for the resort) and coconut groves. And then at last, Maya felt the excitement rise as they laboured up a slope, at the top of which, she knew they would get their first grandstand view of the Arabian Sea.

'Keep your eyes open, we'll be able to see the sea soon!' she told Yash, happy to share the excitement of it with someone. 'The Arabian Sea!' He nodded slowly, warily.

'Thank God!' he drawled, 'for a moment I thought you were going to say Arabian Desert!' She glared at him but couldn't help smiling too. 'There it is!' she exclaimed, pointing out of the window, as if she had been personally responsible for its presence.

It lay there, shimmering in the distance, a gigantic plate of platinum in the late afternoon sun, too bright to look at without squinting, sequins of sunlight bouncing off the waves.

'Just wait,' Maya said, 'in a little while so it'll turn to pure gold! Then you can have all the gold you want right at your feet!'

'So you're a dreamer eh?' he remarked raising his eyebrows again. And added unexpectedly, 'Say which grade are you in? And are you also an only child?'

'No, I have a brother. He's studying in England.' And she wondered how Jayant and Yash would get along together. Probably they wouldn't.

'Oh, then he must be much older than you!'

'He's younger actually. He's what they call a child prodigy! A genius! Tops in whatever he touches!' She hoped he hadn't noticed the bitterness in her voice. She should be proud of Jay dammit, but it just didn't seem to work that way most of the time.

'Oh, one of those! God, you must suffer!' He rolled his eyes again.

'I get by,' she almost whispered, but bit her lip and looked out of the window.

'Bet he can't make up those cool limericks though!' Yash said chortling richly and repeated 'tellible tlolley!' in such a hair-raising accent it made her giggle in spite of herself.

As Srinivas had predicted they drove into Shanbagh at around five-thirty, the sea turning to molten gold as she had said. The resort, spread over about fifteen acres, and shaded by hushing casaurina and coconut trees, was built on the top of a large hillock, simply called 'The Whaleback'. Steps hewn into the cliff-face led down to the beach, which stretched blonde into the distance in both directions in a great curving bow. The resort buildings were built of raw laterite (with wooden window frames and doors), and merged beautifully with their surroundings. The neat red tiles on the roof were weather-beaten just to the right extent, Maya thought, to look comfortable and lived-in and not sterilized as they did in most five-star resorts. Apart from the main villa-style building, which had rooms and suites, there were independent cottages screened behind vivid bougainvillea hedges, scarlet, purple, magenta and white, with big immaculately-maintained lawns in between.

As they drove into the portico, a hefty looking youth of nineteen or twenty with pale watery brown eyes and lank hair emerged holding a camcorder up at his eye. He was wearing baggy grey safari pants and a blue vest cut off at the sleeves, displaying hamlike forearms and unsightly tufts of black hair sprouting from his armpits.

Oh shit, Maya thought uncharitably, with an involuntary shudder, why does Hari have to be the first person we see when we get here? A fair, very attractive girl, in pink shorts and top, with a tiny nose and a mass of dark curls around her head, now flamed gold by the sun, flounced down behind him. She held out her arms and emitted a piglet squeal of delight.

'Chachi! Maya! You've come at last! Welcome to Shanbagh darlings!' As Maya uncoiled from the car, Sherry embraced her and kissed her loudly on both cheeks. 'Guess what? We have the most fabulous beach party organized just for you!' she tinkled, tossing her curls. Hari had come pounding down the steps and stuck his camcorder right into her face.

'And so Miss Maya Sabherwal, will you say a few words about the last Marathon you ran in? And is it true you failed your last dope test and have been disqualified?' He lowered the camera and brayed with laughter.

'Hi Sherry!' Maya stepped back and took a deep breath. Fluffhead or not, Sherry was beautiful. Hari was gross, period.

'No hug for me?' Hari tried to look hurt, then brayed again. As usual there was a pea of grey-green snot glistening in his nostrils, and she stepped back from him, revolted. But he had handed his camera to his sister and was already embracing her mother.

'How are you Pinkie auntie? You're looking so well!' he said, as if he were fifty-five.

'Beta! How big and strong you've grown!' Mrs Sabherwal squawked breathlessly, but pinched his cheek and squeezed his chin affectionately.

'Oh God,' Maya murmured to herself, 'she nearly popped a blackhead there!' And then, her heart sinking rapidly, 'Oh no, now that he's hugged Mama he thinks he can hug me too!' She took yet another step backwards and bumped into the car, but it was too late.

Grinning he stepped forward and wrapped his arms around her crushing himself against her breasts (which were her best part, she believed, rounder and fuller and bouncier than even Sherry's, so there). He kissed her loudly on both cheeks, and hung on, till she wriggled free, almost sick. Out of the corner of her eye she saw Yash raise those woolly bear eyebrows of his again and hide a grin behind his hand. He caught her eye, winked and gave her the thumbs up and stomped off inside behind his parents and the porter wheeling away their luggage. Half pint pipsqueak! Wait till she met him again! She'd have his ears!

'Guess what?' hooted Hari, snatching his camera from Sherry. 'I'm going to be an undercover journalist. And do sting operations!'

Sherry tossed her curls again, knowing the effect they had in this bullion light.

'Ever since Arvind Uncle moved into his villa next door, he's been going on and on about this,' she said, mock-complainingly.

'But really,' said Hari, in that tone of voice that made the bile rise fast in Maya's throat. 'People have a right to know! There's so much evil and crime going on that needs to be exposed. People must see what's happening. Child marriages! Bonded labour! Corruption! You name it! Every politician in this country is neck deep in muck.'

'He wants to impress Arvind Uncle,' said Sherry. 'Hence the social worker-journalist-activist line!'

Mr Arvind Baga was the millionaire head of '*Instantnews!*' an up and coming investigative news and current affairs channel and had caused considerable embarrassment to many politicians through its sting operations. It was also giving the frights to many established news channels. 'And guess what!' Sherry went on, fluttering her eyelashes. 'He wants me to do a screen test as a newsreader! Just imagine!' She giggled. 'But actually I'm keener on modelling. In fact I've got two fabulous modelling assignments already. The team should be coming down to shoot in a few days.' She rolled her eyes. 'I suggested a fabulous location too, and they went gaga when they saw it – not very far from here. But it's great fun!'

'That's great,' Maya mumbled, looking around wildly for escape.

'Beti, where's Papa and Mama?' Mrs Sabherwal asked Sherry, looking around. These two kids would keep them chatting in the porch all evening.

And there was Pankaj Mama at last, bearded, rotund and jovial as ever, very natty in a maroon T-shirt and white Bermudas, as the proprietor of a beach resort should be. He greeted them with affectionate bear hugs, ('my one and only favourite niece!') and turned to her mother.

'But where's that genius boy, Jayant?' he asked, looking around. 'Why haven't you brought him along?'

'Jay is still in England.' Mrs Sabherwal explained proudly. 'But he'll join us here when his holidays start. He just won a big golf tournament and has topped his class in every subject!'

'He's a genius, that fellow. A real genius! Brilliant boy. Really brilliant! You mark my words, he'll win a Nobel prize one day!' Pankaj Mama looked at his watch and turned to his children.

'Hari, Sherry, show Pinkie Auntie and Maya to their cottage and see that they're properly settled and comfortable. Mathew is to look after them, he knows.' He turned to his sister, 'I'm sorry Sadhna could not be here to welcome you; she had to go all the way to Chiplun to see her dentist. She should be back a little later!'

'That's okay, I hope it's not a serious problem!'

'Come along Pinkie Auntie – you'll love the cottage.'

'We go in the car?' Maya asked surprised.

'The family units are about half a kilometre away,' Sherry explained, 'we could walk and they can take the luggage by car, if you like!'

'Or you can run!' Hari bellowed, 'though I don't know which will be faster!' He doubled up with his own wit and quickly put his camcorder up to record her reaction.

But yes, the cottage was beautiful. Of that there was no doubt. Especially after Hari and Sherry had shown them to it and left, (Mrs Sabherwal had said she would like to rest a bit, and Maya said she wanted to settle down and unpack) promising to fetch them for dinner at 8 o'clock. Perched at the top of the hillock, it got a panoramic view of the beach and sea. Like the other buildings it was built of sun-warmed, rusty laterite, with teak window frames and doors. Maya explored the neat cottage, her spirits rising. There were two bedrooms one at each side, with huge attached bath-cum-dressing rooms, a dining-cum-sitting room with a TV, and a lovely verandah that led to a sit-out with a barbeque overlooking the sea. Best of all, it was independent, screened off from other 'family units' (Pankaj Mama had built four) by those ever vibrant and impenetrable bougainvilleas. Thank God, Hari and Sherry stayed with their parents in their own villa, some distance away and so would not be breathing down her neck all the time – what a relief!

After their luggage had been unloaded from the car, Maya went out to the sit-out, and standing at the edge of the stone wall gazed out at the sea, breathing deeply. She loved the sharp briny tang of the wind and the way it brushed back her hair and made her skirt ripple and snap smartly against her legs. As always, she felt that tiny and delicious current of fear course through her as she heard the deep bass boom and thunder of the waves as they curved like molten green glass and broke into a million shards onto the shore, before sweeping in at dangerous speeds, hissing and foaming with malicious delight. In the distance, the sea was still a deep blue, nearer the shore it was more an olive green, laced with froth, excited and agitated. Schizophrenic, Maya thought, placid and quiet one moment, merciless and ferocious the next, sighing sadly one moment, roaring with rage the next. The tide seemed to be in – or coming in fast – she guessed. Even so, a little to the north, three rugged rocky outcrops (and a smaller one next to the one furthest out) reared up, as the waves rushed and leapt around them in frustration. Down on the beach, there were about a dozen yellow and blue beach umbrellas up, and a few (mostly shrimp pink) bathers were whooping it up as they met the breakers with jumps and shouts. But beyond the umbrella zone, stretching both north and south, the blond sands sprawled vast and empty, except for a few stray dogs maybe, freaking out in the shallows. It would be a marvelous beach to run on.

'Madam, in which room should I put your suitcase?' Mathew inquired. He was almost ebony and had the finest, most polished looking skin and whitest teeth Maya had ever seen, not to mention a big beaming smile and sparkling chocolate eyes. His hair was raven black and just as glossy, but neatly trimmed.

'This one thanks,' she said, following him into the veranda and pointing the south-side room. 'Mathew is the tide in now?' she asked.

'Yes, miss, the tide is in.'

'Those rocks there never get covered up?' she asked, pointing to the three islanded rocks.

'No, miss. They are far too high. Actually they are connected by a kind of raised rocky causeway. You know a sort of elevated path runs between the two ridges of rocks on either side. It's like the wall of some sunken fortress. But even those get covered up when the tide comes in.' He smiled, 'So if you are on the rocks when the tide comes in, you have to stay on top of them for around four to five hours to let the sea withdraw from the causeway!'

'And how far out does the tide go?' Maya asked.

'Sometimes it goes all the way back to the third rock, but usually only till the middle rock. But even then, the causeway is uncovered so you can walk right up to the third one. But I don't think you should go so far miss, especially with the monsoon on its way. The sea gets very rough at this time. No one usually goes there.'

'I suppose the beach is safe for swimming?' she asked, suddenly making up her mind that this time, she would indeed swim properly in the sea. It was high time she conquered her silly phobia of getting out of her depth.

'These days you have to be careful miss. Sometimes we get a very strong current sweeping anticlockwise from the south. You see miss, beyond the third rock, there is a reef with an opening to the south, from which the waves begin to sweep in when the tide comes in. So a very strong anticlockwise current is created, and you have to be careful or you can be dashed against the reef and swept over it into open sea.'

Oops, on second thought, maybe it wouldn't be such a good idea to try freestyle swimming just yet, Maya thought, and frowned again. There she was, backing out at the first chance! She smiled at Mathew.

'Thanks, Mathew, I'll keep it in mind!'

'Maya, will you unpack your clothes now!' her mother called petulantly from inside. 'Chatting away all the time!'

'Coming, Ma, I'm not deaf!' She drifted in and wondered idly how Yash was doing. In the veranda, Mathew began laying the table for tea.

She had put on her slinky red miniskirt and black sleeveless top for dinner that night and knew it was a mistake the moment she saw the white golf-cart that Hari had driven up in and announced:

'Madam, your limousine awaits!'

Behind him, Sherry, now in diaphanous peach, giggled and clapped her hands.

Mrs Sabherwal got into the back with Sherry, while she had to squeeze in willy-nilly beside Hari at the front. One hairy thigh and calf was pressed flush against hers, and his ham like arm constantly brushed her own bare arm and shoulder. She wriggled away as far as she could – and almost fell out when he took a turn a little too fast.

'Harry!' screamed Sherry from the back. 'This is not a go-kart you ass!'

'Sorry!' he said. 'Here Maya, shift up closer. You'll fall out!' She could see his teeth glimmer in the dark as he grinned.

Thankfully the journey was short.

A table had been set outside, beside the beautiful sapphire and kingfisher swimming pool, the tablecloth, snow white, the cutlery glittering silver and the glasses twinkling and winking with rainbow reflections.

'So Maya dear, what will you have to drink?' Pankaj Mama boomed, as a big gold and blue wine card was placed deferentially before her. He was a naturally wonderful host (and therefore an excellent hotelier).

'Something soft please, thank you,' she said, glancing around at the other tables. It was still rather early in the evening and just a few were occupied.

'This is so beautiful!' her mother gushed.

'So what are you up to now?' Pankaj Mama asked, after she had ordered her grilled red snapper. Hari, she had noticed was already on his second mug of beer, while Sherry was making merry with her second drink, something tomato red, which she rather cheekily had called a Bloody Mary. Oh yes, of course, that was a vodka drink wasn't it? So Sherry was making merry…

A very pretty girl called Sherry
With vodka was making merry,
She kissed a frog in the pool
And said hey, you big fool
Don't you know that I'm your good fairy!

Sheesh, that was such nonsense, but it had just bubbled up, unstoppable like. But it was strange how Pankaj Mama and Sadhna Mami (who was a pale, mousy lady who didn't seem to participate very much in anything.) didn't raise any objection. Those two were just out of school and were already boozing like there was no tomorrow.

'So Maya, what are you up to now?' her uncle repeated, smiling at her fondly. 'You seem to be back in dreamland…' She looked up startled and embarrassed.

'Oh, I'm so sorry,' she mumbled colouring, 'I was just er… thinking. Er I'm doing nothing very special Mama! Just the usual, school and stuff!'

'Your mother was complaining that you like running too much.' He winked.

'Yes. I enjoy it very much. It… it sort of frees me up…' She smiled and looked down at her plate, which was looking wonderful. 'This looks so good it's a pity one has to eat it!'

'And your genius little brother? Has he decided whether he wants to be an atomic scientist, an astronaut or a cutting-edge brain surgeon?'

'Imagine, he won a major golf tournament at school!' Mrs Sabherwal gushed. 'He beat the seniors hollow. And he's topped in every subject!'

'He does all those sudoku puzzles in under two minutes!' Maya contributed loyally, and making a valiant attempt to put family first. 'He did the last one on the phone! He has a photographic memory.'

'And how long do you take on them?' Hari asked, grinning. 'I don't even look at them. Don't have the patience, besides there are better things to do with your life. But yes, give me a good cause and I'll be there covering it!' He produced his shiny camcorder again and waved it around like a weapon.

'So what are you really into these days, Maya?' Sherry asked, smiling disarmingly. Maya shrugged. It didn't matter what she told Sherry – the girl would forget it in three minutes – she had the attention span of a flea really.

'Oh, nothing really! I like to do a bit of running as I said!'

'She spends all her time running or daydreaming!' Mrs Sabherwal snorted. 'She has not been allowed to sit for her Boards this year and will have to repeat! Just imagine! All she wants to do is run! I'm hoping Jay raja will help her when he comes!'

'Ma, please!'

'You know, those guys from the agency are coming down here soon for the shoot. I can try and get you a screen test. You know dusky is sort of coming back these days.' Sherry said thoughtfully, taking another sip of her drink.

'I don't think I want to model, thanks,' Maya said, turning her attention to her plate, and hoping she was not going too red. She wished the ground would open and swallow her up. She looked away, trying to hide the tear that had suddenly run down her cheek. Then across the pool she spotted Yash and his parents, engrossed in their meal. She pushed her chair back.

'Excuse me, I'll just say hi to a friend,' she said breathlessly, and rose shakily to her feet and quickly looked away as the tears brimmed over.

Pankaj Mama glanced at her and then at his sister. 'Poor kid,' he said softly. 'You shouldn't really have said that she had to repeat the year in front of all of us!'

'But she has to! What can I do? She just doesn't bother with her studies! Put a problem in front of her and she goes phut – completely blank. Put the same problem in front of Jayant and he's like electric current and solves it phatta-phut!'

'Auntie, she'll be all right. She must be feeling bad because Jay has caught up with her in class and gone abroad and is doing so brilliantly.'

'You know she probably has a complex.'

'And you, stupid girl had to go and tell her that dusky is in!' Hari sounded indignant, but it was definitely a snort of laughter that he stifled.

'That's why I wanted her to spend her holidays here. Maybe she'll gain some self-confidence. I think just being here with you all will help.' Mrs Sabherwal looked around gratefully as Pankaj Mama raised his eyebrows.

'Well, we'll do our best Pinkie Auntie!' Hari said a trifle indistinctly. 'You know, actually if this works out it just might make an interesting human interest story… a sort of modern Cinderella tale…'

At the Ahuja's table, Yash's (who had been looking bored to tears) round face lit up when he saw Maya approach. Again, those caterpillar eyebrows shot up.

'Hi,' he greeted her laconically. 'So you are invited to the owner's table, drink the owner's wine and sit next to the owner's son and will now make up limericks about them all on your very first evening! Wow, you mover and shaker, you! Wow!'

She couldn't help laughing at that. What else could you do?

'Shush! You talk too much rubbish Yash!' Mrs Ahuja admonished, smiling at Maya, and noticing the glimmer of tears at once.

'Hi, Uncle, hi Aunty, hi Yash, having a good time?' Maya greeted them somewhat breathlessly, immensely relieved to be away from her own table.

'Hello Maya dear, just ignore him. He can be very rude and precocious! Talks a lot of rubbish!' Mrs Ahuja, still with too much make up on her face took her hand affectionately.

'Why don't you pull up a chair and join us?' Mr Ahuja invited. 'Yash, pull up that chair, please!'

'Thanks,' she said, smiling at Yash, and indicating with a brief nod that she was waiting... Gallantly he rose and pushed the chair in behind her perfectly.

'So you can be a gentleman too!' she commented, grinning.

Normally,' he said, deadpan again, 'normally I pull the chair out when someone sits down, but you make up instant limericks... and right now, the world is in dire need of that!'

'And you keep talking nonsense!' said Mrs Ahuja. Maya looked around and because she was the owner's niece after all felt obliged to ask. 'I hope you're comfortable...?'

'It's beautiful. Better than home and yet not as starched and stuffy as most five star hotels. Your uncle has got the touch just right!'

'I'll tell him that. He'll be very happy!'

'So what are you doing tomorrow?' Yash asked disinterestedly.

'Um I don't know. Go for a run, first thing in the morning I suppose. It's heavenly running on the beach... Then swim maybe or just chill out. I suppose my cousins will have lined up something.' She grimaced at the prospect.

'That will be at some absurd hour I suppose? Your run I mean?'

'Probably!'

'Then I'll see you after that probably.'

She went back to her table after fifteen minutes, smiling shyly and much happier.

'So who's the midget boyfriend?' Hari asked grinning and winking lewdly, 'Woger Wabbit that's shrunk fit?' He snorted and Sherry and let off a shrill peal of laughter that dissolved into giggles and clapped her hands again. She had sneaked a third Bloody Mary when her father had not been looking and it was making itself felt.

Suddenly there was a stir and they looked towards the entrance. Hari suddenly sat up very straight indeed and Sherry ran her hand through her mass of curls.

A distinguished, but wan looking grey-haired man in a sharp dark blue business suit (on the beach, he must be daft, Maya thought) had entered, accompanied by two women. One was obviously his wife, grey-haired like he was and clad in shimmering silk, the second was probably his daughter – a slim slip of a girl, with an oval face and wide-spaced eyes, carrying a bundled up toddler. The man's keen eyes swept across the place, missing nothing, sharp as a ferret's. They made their way slowly towards the Shanbagh's table.

'Hell, that's Arvind Uncle!'

'The lady is his wife, and the stick insect with the toddler is Smita, his daughter!' hissed Sherry, pinching Maya and winking. 'Arvind Uncle's recovering from a major heart attack – and has been here for three weeks!'

Pankaj Mama and Sadhna Mami had risen to their feet to greet their VIP guests.

'Hello Pankaj!' Mr Baga smiled, 'please sit down!'

'Do join us please! How are you feeling now?'

'Restless! Since I can't live at this lovely resort of yours, I thought I'd eat here for a change. I'm sick of my diet.'

'Anything special you need, don't hesitate to ask. Please why don't you join us!'

'Er all right, but just for a little while!'

Another table was brought and joined with theirs and drinks ordered and a round of introductions made. The keen eyes swept the table again.

'Ah, so Hari I see you have your camera ready,' Arvind Baga nodded his head. 'Good boy! You never know when a story might unfold!'

'Always at the ready, that's me. I hope to have a scoop for *'Instantnews!'* at any time.'

'Uncle, he's quite a pest really. Always stuffing that camera into people's faces and asking personal questions!' Sherry complained.

Mr Baga nodded and turned to Pankaj Mama. 'Actually, Pankaj I was talking to the features team this morning. They want to do a feature on the best beach resorts of India, so I suggested why not start here. You have a truly lovely place out here.'

'That's an excellent idea. You are welcome at any time! Just give us a day's notice so we can make sure the crabs and lobsters are fresh!'

'Okay, then that's fixed. I think the team should be able to drive down in four or five days time. I've been pushing them very hard and they will enjoy a break of this kind!'

'Any time, sir, any time!' said Pankaj Mama expansively. He knew it would be good publicity, though you had to watch out for these self-styled investigative types. Always raking up unexpected, unpleasant surprises. Still, with Baga sahib having a good time – and a plush villa just next door – he didn't think there would be any problem.

Maya, sitting next to stick insect Smita, looked at the sleeping baby.

'Is it a boy or girl?' she asked, smiling.

'A girl,' said the mother. 'Her name's Asha! She's nine months old.'

'She's so sweet!' Maya looked around surprised that there was no ayah and that the mother had lugged along a huge bag presumably full of what babies needed when they had late nights.

'So Sherry dear, I believe you've gone into modelling?' Mrs Baga asked Sherry who turned a searchlight smile on the lady.

'Yes, Auntie, I have a shoot scheduled for next week. They're paying me twenty-five grand, for maybe two days' work can you believe it! They must be crazy!'

'And... er Maya, and what are you doing?' the great Mr Baga was suddenly asking her.

'Oh me?' Maya looked around. 'Er... I'm in school and just here for a holiday, sir!' she said.

'Good! That's the most sensible thing I've heard all evening!' the great man said and Maya blushed, hoping this time her mother would keep her mouth shut for once and that this was not just polite conversation on the part of Mr Baga, which it probably was.

The Bagas left soon after, and then Mr and Mrs Ahuja and Yash came over to say goodnight.

'You have a wonderful place here,' Mrs Ahuja said. 'It's the friendliest place we've been to in a very long time.'

'And excellent food!'

As Maya introduced Yash to her cousins…

'Sherry, Hari this is Yash Ahuja. We drove down together from Bombay this morning. Yash these are my cousins, Hari and Sherry.' She held her breath hoping Yash would not come out with some horribly embarrassing wisecrack.

'Hi Yash,' Sherry was friendly enough but Hari had a peculiar look in his eye.

'So Yash, what do you like to do in your spare time?' he asked, stretching his arms and yawning. 'Play Tom Thumb?'

'Oh, hang around, mess about! Yup and that also!'

'Did you know,' Hari said seriously, 'if you hang from a branch for ten minutes every day you can gain three inches in height in a month's time?'

Yash nodded, deadpan. 'Yes and I suppose if you hang for ten or fifteen hours a day, you can become an orangutan with hairy and smelly armpits in no time at all!'

Maya choked back a sudden giggle and glared at Yash, but he raised a quizzical eyebrow at her and walked off behind his parents.

'What did the little midget mean by that?' Hari spluttered, puzzled and sniffing at his armpits.

'Hari!' Sherry squealed. 'Please, not at the table. We've just eaten!'

It was past ten-thirty by the time the party broke up.

'Come on, I'll drive you back,' offered Hari after they had said their goodnights and thank yous to their hosts.

'I think I'll walk,' Maya decided, not wanting another ride up front with Hari. 'It's such a lovely night.'

'Don't be silly Maya, come on!' Mrs Sabherwal exclaimed, settling herself into the wretched golf cart, as a rather giggly (and rather sleepy) Sherry squeezed in beside her. 'It's too far and quite dark and you don't know the way. There may be snakes!'

'Um... maybe it would be better if you came with us,' Hari agreed, nodding. 'It's quite a winding path and you can get lost!'

There was nothing for it, but to get in again, and feel that hairy leg press against her own smooth one. Idiot that she was, wearing this short skirt with this letch around. He was steering with one hand now and quite casually put his other hand on her thigh and squeezed it. She stiffened and snatched his hand off.

'Stop it!' she hissed. 'Please stop it!'

'Sorry,' he grinned, 'I thought that was the handbrake!'

At last they arrived and Mrs Sabherwal disembarked from the rear.

'Thank you beta,' she said. 'Poor Sherry has fallen asleep. You better take her home. Come on now Maya.' She turned and surged up the steps.

And Maya, who had virtually leapt off, discovered that she had dropped her little black purse while pushing Hari's hand off her thigh. She groped around in the footwell and under the seat, feeling around for it.

'Dropped something – here let me help you.'

Hari half lay down on the front seat and hung his hand down as if to search beneath it, and stared at her bare arm and shoulder now inches from his face. To her horror she suddenly felt fingers crawl inside her top up from her midriff and close around her left breast. As if bitten, she drew back, hitting her head against the bulkhead, and stumbled to her feet.

'Please, stop it will you!' She was almost in tears, and rubbed her head. Hari got off the seat, a grin on his face and with a magician's flourish, produced the little black purse.

'Found it! Here you are!'

'Thanks!' She snatched it from him and turned to go.

'Okay, okay, no need to get so uptight,' he said unflappably. At the back, Sherry was still sound asleep and snoring softly now. And then let loose his final goodnight barb. 'You know, you should be grateful for small mercies, Maya!' he whispered softly.

She stormed off into the cottage, choking back her sobs, her skirt swinging around her hips, as he watched her go and leered. Then, he took out a cigarette and lit it casually and drove off. It was going to be an interesting summer.

She should have slapped him, of course, hard and tight. Screamed and slapped him good and proper and scratched his hateful face. Instead she had weakly squealed, 'please, stop it!' like some helpless simpering female in a Hindi film.

But what was worst was that last insult, like the sting of a Portuguese Man O'War. It echoed mockingly and burned in her head till late that night. 'You should be grateful for small mercies, Maya!' Unable to sleep, she walked to the sit-out, and gazed at the sea.

The tide had drawn way back, and the sea was hushing and whispering – consolingly she thought – its lacy frill of foam, glimmering ghostily in the starlight. The air smelt briny and of all the things the sea had forgotten and left behind, some nice, some not so nice.

And just before she went in to sleep, she whispered the words of the first of the black limericks that would plague her that summer:

The sea breeze is briny tonight
And the king prawns were such a delight
But there's a letch in this place
I should have spat in his face
And certainly slapped good & tight!

3

She was up by five-thirty the next morning, and like the new tide sweeping away the detritus left behind by the old, the horror and unpleasantness of the previous night had been rinsed clean away from her mind. A steady cool breeze blew in from the sea, a dark grey-blue in the pre-dawn light. Far out on the rim of the horizon she could see the pinprick lights of a ship, drifting slowly northwards – towards Mumbai probably – with whatever cargo it was carrying. And closer to the shore, a long line of ant-like black dots bobbing – fishing boats.

'It's so beautiful,' Maya thought, breathing in deeply. Quickly she put on her white running shorts and a sunny yellow T-shirt, and debated whether to run barefoot or not. In the end she decided to put on her sneakers – she could always take them off if she wanted to later on. She did her warming up exercises thoroughly on the sit-out and then opened the little red gate at the edge of the garden. The steps, hewn out of rock, were steep, but she went down them lightly, and then was out on the beach. With an exasperated, 'Nah!' she unlaced her shoes, and tucked them behind a rock at the base of the steps. The sand was deliciously cool and she wriggled her toes ecstatically in them. She picked her way carefully amidst the fearsome spinifex and then was out on the firm cool sand. In both directions, the beach stretched, vast and empty – it was all hers.

And then she was running. It took her a few minutes to get the feel of the surface, but soon she was loping gracefully along and feeling as usual that she could go on forever. Happily she splashed through the shallow tide pools that awaited the sea again, nimbly dodging the stranded green and purple Portuguese man o'war and mentally apologizing to the crabs that scuttled indignantly out of her way as she thudded past. Small streams trickled down occasionally from the leeward side, and she splashed through these too, revelling in the coolness of the water splashing up from underfoot. It was heaven. Within five minutes she had achieved that trance-like state, which she liked to think was as close to nirvana as you could get. She was in her element, a runner doing her thing (or so she liked to think). And so she ran and ran, graceful, at ease and sublime, every sinew happy to be working.

Up ahead, she noticed she was approaching what was probably a fishing village. She could see the boats drawn up on the beach, and she glanced at the sea and saw that the fleet appeared to be returning. She had to watch where she put her feet now, there was more rubbish strewn on the beach, driftwood smoothened by the sea, tattered bits of nylon netting, crushed plastic bottles and gleaming shards of glass, licked smooth by the sea, but still dangerous and of course, the occasional potty, human and canine. Men, women and children were coming out on the beach to meet the incoming boats, with baskets and plastic containers. She had been running for about fifteen minutes now, slower than when she had started out, and realizing that running on sand (no matter how firm) was more tiring than running on grass or on a track. She was sweating freely, but her face was cool in the tangy breeze. As she drew close to the village, a clutch of small boys with flapping shorts full of holes came running out to greet her, beaming, shouting and waving.

'Madam want fish?'

'Madam wants shells? Beautiful shells, I have!'

'Madam is champion Olumpic runner?'

The women, with their colourful tucked-up saris, glanced at her, some surly faced, some smiling toothily. But they were more preoccupied with the boats, the first of which had just come ashore.

The leapt into the shallows, and helped the men drag the heavy boats in. Smiling shyly, Maya ran through the village and beyond, skipping neatly over obstacles and to her delight, the clutch of small boys followed on her heels. Some raced ahead, at top speed, yelling with delight that they had beaten this 'champion runner memsab', but soon they fell back as Maya ran on and on. She turned around at last, and was surprised to note how far she had come. The resort was not visible from here, hidden behind the coconut and casuarinas, but she recognized Whaleback hillock and the three rocks that 'marched into the sea'. They looked quite insignificant.

She jogged slowly back through the village again, noticing that a knot of people had gathered around the fisherfolk, and realized that an impromptu fish market was being held. (A daily occurrence, shc was to discover.) This time just one little boy joined her, running valiantly beside her, his black eyes shining.

'Myself Sushant,' he introduced himself perkily, 'Madam, want cowries? Beautiful cowries I have!' Still running he held up his hand, and automatically Maya took what he was offering, feeling the clink of shells in her palm. Six large, glossy, lacquered chocolate brown cowries beautifully patterned with circular nuggets of gold, gleamed up at her. They were exquisite. Astonished she stopped and gazed at them, panting.

'Chocolate cowries madam, my father bringing all the way from Kutch! With pure gold in them! 22-carat gold!'

'They're beautiful, but I don't have any money,' she said, examining them closely. They glowed back at her alluringly. Reluctantly she handed them back.

'Never mind, you bring money tomorrow!'

'How much?'

'Only fifty rupees!'

'Fifty rupees?'

'Okay, then forty!'

'Ten!'

'Thirty!'

'Fifteen! That's all, now I have to go!'

'Okay, madam, deal! But you are starving me!'

But the little imp had stuck out his hand to shake on the deal.

Laughingly she shook it and ran on. 'Done!' she yelled. 'I'll bring the money tomorrow morning!'

'I show you more shells tomorrow! All shapes, all colours, all beautiful!'

Obviously, the little boys from this village had been doing good business with the holidaymakers that stayed at Shanbagh Resort.

She was deliciously deadbeat by the time she got back to the resort. It was just getting on to around 7 o'clock, and a few people were on the beach, walking or swimming. To her surprise she spotted Smita playing with her little daughter at the edge of the tide line. The baby, who had a bouncy mass of curls – rather like Sherry, thought Maya – and round button eyes had dayglo orange floaters strapped to her chubby arms and thighs and was screaming with delight as the waves hissed in and splashed her. Panting Maya drew up and collapsed on the sand nearby.

'Hi Smita,' she said. 'She's really enjoying herself, isn't she?'

Smita looked around and smiled proudly. 'Oh, hi! Yes,' she said. 'She just loves the water. And she's absolutely fearless. Most kids scream and run when they see the waves coming in, this one wants to take them head on like a baby turtle!'

She seems nice, Maya thought, again surprised that there was no ayah around to look after the baby.

'She's sweet!' she said, holding out her hand to the baby. Asha grabbed it hard and grinned up at her.

'I really have to watch her,' Smita said. 'Leave her on her own and she runs straight into the sea as if she wants to swim to Africa!'

Maya got to her feet. 'I'd better put a wrap on,' she said. 'I'm sweating like a horse. I'd love to play with her some time!'

'She'd love it! I'm down here most mornings. She's an early riser! You can join us anytime!'

'Thanks! I will! Bye then, see you later Smita! Bye Asha!'

At the cottage, Mathew had just brought up the bed tea and asked whether they would be breakfasting in the sit-out or the dining hall.

'We'll eat here, Mathew,' Mrs Sabherwal said, much to Maya's relief.

'Oof Ma, I'm pooped and famished!' Maya said, collapsing into the lovely cane recliners at the edge of the sit-out. 'I had a wonderful run! And see what I got!' She took out her beautiful shells.

'Running already, eh? You must have been a horse in your last life I tell you. Always running!'

'Yes, Ma!' Maya agreed dreamily, relishing the ice-cold orange juice that Mathew had produced like magic. 'A racehorse probably! A Derby winner!'

She just loved the languid dream-like fatigue and ache that came after a good run. Once you got your wind under control (which she did very quickly indeed) your muscles felt as if they had been massaged by heaven. After a while, she went in for a shower and emerged fresh and chirpy – and gasped.

Out in the sit-out, Mathew had laid out a breakfast of magnificent proportions.

'That… that's not a papaya, Mathew,' Maya said weakly, 'that's an entire sunset!' Papaya apart, there was a huge pile of butter yellow scrambled eggs, slices of pink ham cut paper thin, a heap of golden toast like a pile of crisp leaves, four squat jars of different jams and marmalades and of course, cornflakes and milk and a huge pot of coffee that made her nose twitch ecstatically. Not to mention a heap of fluffy white idlis and two huge crisp dosas surrounded by their flotillas of chutneys and sambar.

'I'm going to put on weight here even before lunch!' Maya groaned, as she tucked in hungrily.

'So what are you doing the rest of the day?' her mother asked. 'Now that you've had your run.'

'I don't know, Ma.' She made a face. 'Probably hang out with Sherry and Hari!'

Mathew, who had been clearing up the breakfast things, cleared his throat.

'Er... miss, Sherry ma'am has sent a message that she has a terrible migraine (a hangover really) and will remain in bed all day. Hari sir said he has to go and meet Mr Baga about fixing things for the television people's visit.' And actually, Hari was a little afraid that Maya might have complained to her mother about what had happened last night – he wanted to let a little time pass before he dared show his face again. But if she hadn't tattled...

Maya's face lit up. Oh joy! What a relief! She supposed she could go and see how Sherry was sometime later, but she had pretty much the whole day to herself.

I'll go for a swim and then check out those rocks, they look interesting, all jagged and rugged, she decided. 'Ma,' she called out, 'I'm going down to the beach. Will you put on some sun tan lotion on me, please?'

'Don't stay out in the sun too long. And don't go into the sea. What time will you be back?'

'Ma, really! We're at the beach! We're on a holiday! What difference does it matter what time it is!'

Quickly – before her mother could come up with some awful suggestion as to how she could spend the day – she changed into her bottle green swimsuit and draped her toweling coat over her shoulder. She slipped on her flip-flops put on a straw hat, and with a brisk, 'Bye, Ma!' was out of the gate and down the steps again.

There were more people on the beach now, and the tide was pulling out. Recliners had been laid out, and prawn-pink foreigners were lying in the sun like walruses drying out. The receding tide had left a huge shimmering bow shaped pool of water along the beach and Maya remembered what Mathew had told her about the counter clockwise current that swept round the beach. Maybe the huge pool was what it had left behind. She was surprised to find no sign of Yash and his parents on the beach, she had been half-hoping to meet him, but was not really disappointed because she was accustomed to being by herself. She looked at the tide line and nodded.

'Ah, Maya my girl stop dithering and take on your challenge!' she told herself firmly, trying to quell the nervousness rising in the pit of her stomach. She nodded decisively.

Yes, she would swim in the sea properly – out of her depth.

She placed her robe, slippers and hat on the beach and headed out to sea with a determined step. At first she thought – and hoped – that the pool left by the tide would be deep enough for her to try her experiment. But the water, still and clear and warm, was only knee deep at its deepest. There was no choice, but to head directly out to sea!

Tentatively she waded in, watching as the water came up first to her knees and then her thighs and hips. The waves, which had lost their power and arrogance, still nudged and pushed her this way and that, she could sense the incipient power of the glassy swells as they curled and collapsed. She was deep enough now to feel the buoyancy of the water to try to lift her, but kept her feet planted firmly at the bottom, parting the water with her hands. She shut her eyes and murmured:

Maya went for a swim in the sea
And tried hard not to turn back and flee
The waves nudged her gently,
And said will you kindly
Just get off your feet and float free!

She smiled wanly wondering what Yash's reaction to that would have been. Okay, let yourself go! Just one more step and then I'll draw up my legs and tread water and launch into freestyle all the way to Madagascar! She stepped forward and floundered as the ground suddenly and horribly disappeared beneath her feet. She fell headlong, her arms spread-eagled and splashing, then tumbled right over, somersaulting, kicking wildly with her legs. She bobbed up, now flat on her back as the waves maliciously slopped gallons of water into her mouth and up her nose. She could feel the enormous easy power of the swells as they lifted her as if rocking a baby. Desperately she trod water and much to her horror could not feel the seabed beneath her stretched out toes. She swallowed and coughed again, as the sea lifted and dipped her at will.

And panicked again; oh God, she was caught in a current and would be swept out to Madagascar in two minutes flat or smashed to a pulp on the reef! But then thank God, she could suddenly feel the bottom again beneath her feet. Gasping, almost chin deep now righted herself and pushed slowly shore wards, realizing what had happened. The beach had dipped suddenly and risen again – she had simply stepped into a trench as it were and right out of her depth. But now, to get back to shore she had to step over that dip or crevasse (that's what it was, a damn crevasse, lurking there to trap the unwary!) again. There was nothing for it; willy-nilly she had to cross it again to get safely back to the beach. She turned around facing the beach, took a deep breath and dipped her head beneath the water, trying to spot the trench, but it was just too murky. Spluttering and with smarting eyes, she took her head out again and wiped the water and hair back from her face.

'Okay, I know it's there, so I'll just feel for the edge, with my feet!' She took a small step forward, and felt herself being pushed back towards open sea by the retreating tide. But then she found it, as her toes clenched suddenly and she teetered. With a squawk she launched herself forwards, taking as large a step as she could like someone stepping over a large ditch. And much to her relief found she was on terra firma again, so to speak, the 'trench' was just about three feet across. The sea was rushing back now, the water splashing up against her thighs, but getting shallower with every step. Gasping, she waded out, wondering how many gallons of seawater she had swallowed. So much for her freestyle swim to Madagascar, she thought wryly. If only that stupid trench had not been there. But this beach was tricky and dangerous – it had traps and currents hidden everywhere. And Maya shelved her grand plans for swimming for the time being, even though a small and nagging voice inside told her that she ought to try again.

'Not today!' she said out loud. 'Not today!' And might well have said, 'not ever'. 'I'm just going to laze about and have a good time,' she decided. 'This is a holiday, dammit not some sort of test your courage exercise. She collected her flip-flops and robe and headed towards the first of the big rocks, which had more or less been marooned by the receding tide.

As Mathew had mentioned, the three rocks were linked together by a causeway formed by two parallel ridges of rocks that started from high up on the beach – beyond even the high-tide mark. Maya just walked up to the ridge 'wall' closest to her, and clambered over it carefully. They were pitted and jagged, and studded with razor-sharp barnacles and she was grateful she had her slippers with her, though ideally rubber-soled sneakers would have been better, she thought. Carefully she made her way over the ridge, into the causeway and looked around. Dark moss-green rock pools glinted in the sunlight, some wearing a frill of foam around their edges. In between them were pleasant sandy patches too where the crabs scuttled sideways and dug themselves in hurriedly as she approached. She threaded her way between the small rocks and boulders easily and soon was clambering nimbly over the first of the big rocks, then down it and on to the causeway at its far side.

'This is great!' she said peering over the ridge, where the sea still sucked and gurgled malevolently but ineffectively (like a gargling giant, she thought), because it was draining back. She climbed over and across the second rock too, which was easier than the first had been, completely dry now and sweating, because the sun was up and strong. By now, she knew which type of moss was slimy and must be avoided and which felt like velvet and could be trusted, though not too much. Many of the rocks – one of which she had inadvertently laid a hand on and cut her palm – were sharp as rusted razors and had to be traversed with the utmost care.

'Razor rocks, that's what I'll call them,' she decided. Razor Rocks 1, 2 and 3.

And it was Razor Rock 3 that made her exploration completely worthwhile. It was the biggest of the three, rearing up almost fifty-feet high, and about the same length from end to end. At its broadest part it was about thirty feet across.

'An islet, really,' Maya thought. 'But Razor Rock 3, it's going to remain!' Just off its north side, across a tumultuous channel twenty or thirty-feet wide, another small rock jutted proudly out. 'Little Rock' of course, Maya thought delighted.

At the base of Rock 3, Maya looked up, figuring out whether it was climbable. It seemed to be. Though at some places it was almost a vertical climb up the rock face, it was easy to hoist oneself up because the rocks had been sort of stacked up one on top of another very conveniently. 'They're like a staircase for a giant,' Maya thought panting as she hauled herself up. And the climb was worth it. From the top of Razor Rock 3 you got a magnificent view. The beach was some 700 or 800 metres (or was it more?) away, (she guessed) blindingly white, the bathers and tourists, mere specks. Around the islet the sea nuzzled and gurgled and made horrible sucking noises as it swirled forwards and then drew back. Ducking low because she didn't want to be spotted by anyone on the beach (who would probably have a panic attack) she made her way towards the seaward edge of the rock. Some distance ahead, she could see the frill of foam and veil of spume, where the breakers hit the reef that Mathew had mentioned. Which made the waters immediately in front of the Razor Rock 3 and those to its south side, lagoon calm – but more cunning she wondered, not willing to trust the sea again. But this was heaven – Maya was sure no one ever came all the way up here – it had been hot and hard work clambering up and over those blade-dangerous rocks. And then she glanced down and saw the hidden sandy cove.

Beautifully sheltered, shaped and patterned by the sea's craftsmanship, like a scallop, it was completely hidden from view, with clear glinting water lapping gently, the sand glimmering silvery beneath. She clambered down quickly, pausing to take note of the wide rocky overhang and ledge about halfway down. 'Nice place to sit,' she thought continuing on her way. Landing lightly on the sand, she took off her slippers and robe, tucking them behind a rock. It would desecrate the place to wear footwear here, she thought. The little cove, more like a large sand-bottomed pool, was divine. Pale pink and dark-green elongated shells, thin as wafers, lay scattered about, as did starfish, most still alive, waving their tentacles slowly. She lay down in the water, relishing its coolness. A cove for just one or two persons, she thought. No more. This is going to be my big secret. The sea entered the cove from the south, through a wide channel when the tide came in, gushing over widely spaced rocks that slowed, and calmed them down considerably ('speedbreakers' Maya thought delightedly). Three sides of the cove were guarded by jagged rocky outcrops (like the pincers of some monster crustacean!) – the fourth – looked out to open sea.

'Wow!' Maya exulted. 'I have my own private beach! I can sunbathe in the nude here if I want!' But she knew she'd never do that. She wasn't even too bothered by the huge green crabs she spotted clattering over the rocks and was delighted as tiny silver fish darted in and nibbled at (and between) her rose-pink toes, rolling their beady eyes at her.

'I can bring stuff here to eat and drink and a book' she planned. 'And spend the whole day pottering about or lolling! All I need to do is to keep track of the tide. And even if it does come in, I'll be safe! I'll simply climb up to that ledge there!' Though she could imagine her mother's hysterics if she went missing for six hours or was spotted on top of the rock! Still it would be fun to be 'stranded' here when the tide was high, just for the experience…

She lolled happily in the shallows, even swam freestyle in the swimming-pool-calm water, (though really it was not 'out of her depth') and floated on her back. It was heavenly. She dozed off and slumbered for a while, before waking with a start. Burned brown and deliciously dozy and ravenous, she reluctantly thought about getting back. Her mother would of course, kick up a huge fuss if she were late for lunch. If she weren't already late for lunch, in which case it didn't matter provided she was in time for tea!

'Heck, I'm thinking like I'm drunk! I've had too much sun!' she giggled, as another limerick began to stir. Suddenly she stiffened and cocked her head. Was that a voice? Accompanied by the clattering of a rock?

There was someone else in her private paradise.

'Oh shit!' Suddenly a small flame of fear flickered deep inside her. This was not the ideal place to be stranded with a stranger. Stupid girl, it would probably be only some other visitor at the resort – who else would come here? Still cautious she glanced around and ducked behind a huge overhanging rock that prevented her from being seen from above and waited. Hopefully the person would just potter around and then leave. But damn, she'd left daisy chains of footmarks all over the sandy cove – and her slippers and toweling coat, folded neatly on that rock. It was too late to do anything about them.

'Heeyaah! I'm the Cannibal King!' She nearly shrieked with fright as the sturdy dumpy figure clad in flapping red trunks came flying down and landed with a thump on the sand as if from the sky itself and then began a wild war dance, singing at the top of its voice. It had a shock of black hair standing straight up from the forehead, and a baseball cap was being waved like a club:

The cannibal king, with the big nose ring
Fell in love with a dusky maayydenn!
And in the pale moonlight, by the river side
He danced with his dusky maayyden!
Barooom! Baroom! Baroombilliaeeyay-ay-ay!
Barooom! Barooom! Barooombilliaeeyay!

The song stopped suddenly as the singer's eye fell on Maya's footprints and her purple flip-flops and robe neatly parked behind their rock.

Doubled up with laughter, Maya emerged from her hiding place. Poor Yash was still standing rooted staring at her footprints, his back to her.

'Hail oh Cannibal King! Do you always jump out of the sky singing about dusky maidens?' she snorted and dissolved into helpless giggles and then staggered around in stitches.

'Yaaagh!' Startled he jumped around and then mopped his brow.

'My God, it's only you! I thought it was some evil siren from the sea coming to drag me into the depths!' But his face and ears were turning scarlet with embarrassment.

'You're too much Yash, sing that again!' she pleaded doubling up again. 'Please! I haven't heard that version before!'

But he was having none of it. 'Say how long have you been here?' he asked indicating the footprints. 'All day?'

'Um, well quite a while! I was thinking of getting back. My mom will throw a fit. But isn't it lovely!'

He grinned and glanced around and nodded. 'Cool isn't it? I don't think anyone comes here.'

She grinned. 'Except Cannibal Kings singing about dusky maidens! Anyway let's keep it that way, shall we?'

'Done, it's our secret hideout then! Let's swear on it. Cross my heart and hope to die!'

'Me too! Did you bring anything to eat? I'm famished.'

'I always carry rations!' he said with dignity. 'I left the rucksack on top of the rock.' He was lying down in the water now, and suddenly grinned. 'Say, you made up any more of those cool limerick things again?' He frowned. 'Oh by the way, that big snotty lout at the resort was looking around and shouting for you…'

'Oh… you mean Hari. He's my cousin by the way!'

'Sorry. I know. But he's still gross! Poking that stupid camera in your face all the time, asking stupid questions.' He mimicked Hari's sanctimonious voice beautifully. 'And what wonderful memories of this place will you carrying back with you when you return?'

She grinned wickedly as the limerick popped up rough but readymade:

There was a big lout called Harry
Who filmed a naked big Mammy
Big Mammy got wild
And said come here child
And hurt dirty Harry quite badly!

Yash stared at her his eyes goggling. And then let loose a piercing screech, and whooped and whistled hysterical with laughter. 'That's just too much! Just how do you do it?' He was rolling about in the sand holding his sides. '*Hurt dirty Harry very badly*, oh my God! Oh my God! You're just too much!'

She grinned at him, delighted, but wished that she had been just a little bit like Big Mammy last night. Still it made her glow warmly; it was just so wonderful that at least one person liked her limericks so much and, 'so spontaneously'. Her friends thought she was weird. Gross. Seventeen-year-old girls did not make up limericks. Period. Bah!

'Come on,' she said. 'What have you brought to eat?'

They climbed up to the top of the rock, where Yash had left his knapsack. He delved in it and took out a couple of granola bars. They chewed on their bars in companionable silence, the stiff sea breeze cooling them.

Then Yash glanced at her and delved into his knapsack again and casually took out a new pack of cigarettes. He broke it open and pulled out a stick.

'Smoke?' he asked, offering it to Maya.

'What? No! No thanks!'

He pulled out the stick and dangled it at the corner of his mouth, stuffing the pack back into the knapsack. He took out a matchbox and struck a light. It flared, and the wind whipped it out. He was successful at last at his sixth attempt, cupping his hands low over it before taking a deep, relieved drag and flicking it out.

And reeled backwards in a paroxysm of hacking and coughing, his face turning bright red, his eyes watering copiously.

'Da... damn smoke went down the wrong way!' he spluttered and she grinned wondering 'and which way would that be you goose?'

'Here, let me help you Mr Marlboro Man!' she said kindly, hiding her grin and thumping him gently on the back. 'Easy!'

'I'm fine!' he spluttered, eyeing the cigarette as if it had just bitten him. 'Really, I am!' He put it to his lips again and took another drag. Only to be sent staggering backwards again as a fresh bout of coughing racked him.

'Hey, take it easy! You're obviously allergic to this brand!' she said gently. And added to herself, 'And have never had a smoke in your life before you silly goose but thanks for trying to impress me anyway, I'm flattered!'

'Ye... yeah it must be that!' he said stubbing out the wretched thing with alacrity. 'Some foul local brand, probably fake too!'

'Probably!' For a moment he looked at her suspiciously, but her smoky eyes were wide and grave.

'Come on,' she said, 'we'd better get back!'

'You know,' he said casually, dusting his hands on his trunks and giving her a sidelong glance. 'You look real hot in a swimsuit. Great boo... er figure... er whatever, you know what I mean!'

'What?' She looked down hastily and realized that the top half of her breasts were bared and most of her cleavage exposed. Hastily she hitched her swimsuit up, and slipped on her coat, tucking in snugly around her, colouring. The cheeky little pipsqueak!

'Sorry if I offended you,' he said, not sounding in the least sorry. 'I meant it for the best.'

'Hmph,' she snorted lunging for his ear and twisting it gently. 'And just how many times have you tried this line, mister half-pint?'

He grinned. 'On every chickie I meet,' he admitted. 'Now let's go!'

'You must have got slapped plenty!'

He grinned again. 'Sort of,' he admitted, leaping down from rock to rock.

'Watch it,' she yelled. 'Those rocks are like sharks' teeth!'

They made their way back slowly up the 'causeway'. At some point the tide had turned and she could sense the fresh urgency as the waves raced in, foaming eagerly. Occasionally they swished over the causeway ridge, spilling water inside, but it would take some time before the causeway flooded up.

Neither of them noticed Hari Shanbagh up on Rock 1, crouched behind a boulder his camcorder at his eye. Earlier that morning he had realized that Maya had obviously not complained about last night to her mother. In fact Pinkie Auntie had requested him to look for her, when she had not turned up for lunch. He had searched the resort thoroughly, and scoured the beach too, but hadn't thought about the rocks. Disgruntled he had taken his camera and hidden himself behind a boulder on Razor Rock 1, his gaze on the beach. Sometimes very famous people (Hollywood actors even) stayed at the resort, and sunbathed and he got his kicks by filming them secretly. Like the paparazzi, he liked to think. Who knew, one day he might catch some beautiful and famous actress with someone she was not meant to be with, and better still, topless. He'd make millions selling his pictures around the world! He had wondered where Maya had disappeared and thought she might have gone for a run, though this was a stupid time for that. Then he heard voices floating in from the sea behind him and turned around.

Oh ho! So that's where she had been – hiding behind those rocks. And with her midget boyfriend too! God knows what they had been doing behind the rocks. A rather cunning look came over his face, accompanied by an unpleasant smirk. Anyway, now he knew where to look for her. He patted his camera. 'You and I are going to have a good time, I think, my friend' he murmured and raised it to his eye. But they weren't even holding hands so he zoomed in on Maya. He took a fifteen second burst, and knew that he would have to reveal himself as they approached or be spotted. So he put the camera into his belt bag, stood up and waved.

'Maya! Where have you been? Your mom is looking for you!'

Startled, Maya and Yash looked up.

'Oh shit, it's that creep!' Maya waved back.

'Coming!' she called. 'What's the problem?'

'You didn't show up for lunch and she was worried! You should have told her, you know.'

'Lunch? What time is it?'

'Almost four! I've been looking all over for you!'

'But I told her where I was going!'

They had reached Rock 1 and he joined them. 'Really, you shouldn't disappear for so long,' he said shaking his head like a disapproving elder brother. He glanced at Yash but said nothing.

'I guess I lost track of the time,' Maya admitted.

He took her arm and squeezed it. 'That happens,' he said with mock sympathy. 'But maybe you should be more careful. Next time I'll come along with you. Come on, now.' The arm snaked around her waist, but she drew aside quickly.

'Bye Maya,' Yash called, raising his damn eyebrows again. 'Have a nice evening!'

'See you,' she said, and smiled. Suddenly she realized that she was dead tired and still very hungry.

'But Ma, I told you where I was going. I can't help it if you don't listen!'

'I don't care! You should have been home for lunch. Or told me!'

'How? You won't let me have a cellphone!'

'I don't care! I was so worried! Running about all alone god knows where!'

'Really there was nothing to worry about. And I was with that little boy – Yash – who we met yesterday! So there!'

'You better stay here now. We're dining with Pankaj Mama and Sadhna Mami at their place tonight.'

She made a face. 'Do I have to come? I'm really tired.'

'Of course you have to! You can rest now! There's plenty of time!'

The Shanbagh's villa was set in its own grounds some distance away from the 'Family Plot' (as Pankaj Mama called their clutch of four cottages). It was an elegant looking house, with sloping tiled roofs, long bougainvillea-shrouded verandas all around, and an open courtyard inside.

Thankfully, this time it was Mathew who turned up in the golf cart to drive them the few hundred yards. The table had been set around the small pool, because it was a balmy night again – and anyway huge pedestal fans whirred nonstop.

'Pinkie Auntie, what a beautiful sari! Maya darling where have you been all day, you naughty girl!' With a tinkling laugh (like breaking glass, Maya thought) Sherry took her arm and kissed her. 'Just look at you! One day here and you already have a tan to die for! Oh, I'm so jealous!'

'So how's your headache?' Maya asked. 'I hope you're feeling better!'

Sherry screwed up her pert nose. 'I'll live darling, I'll live! Now listen, I have something fabulous to tell you. You know the guys from the ad firm are driving down tomorrow for the shoot. They need evening shots – on the beach of course. So I'd love it if you come along – who knows, Arunda might just take a fancy and sign you up for a screen test.' She pealed again, 'Just imagine you might be the next big thing in modelling darling!'

Then Hari arrived talking on his cellphone. He put it away and waved at Maya.

'So Sherry it's all fixed up!' he called. 'The party's on! Day after tomorrow! At Billy's place down on his beach.'

'Now we'll have to ask Papa if he'll agree to arrange the food and booze,' Sherry said mock-conspiratorially, screwing up her nose (No wonder it was all scrunched up, Maya thought). She turned to Maya and batted her eyelashes. 'And of course, you're invited – you have to come, you're the guest of honour! And bring that cute little boyfriend of yours along too! Some friends from Bombay will be joining us too! It'll be great!'

Maya blushed and was about to protest, when she stopped herself. It wouldn't make any difference – they wouldn't hear anything – they never listened. She settled down to do justice to the huge helping of prawn and shrimp curry on her plate. To her pleasant surprise, Hari didn't try anything funny – he was exquisitely polite – jumping out of his place and helping her mother to sit, passing the dishes around, smiling warmly, and murmuring 'My pleasure, my pleasure!' He didn't even sit next to her at the table, nor did he try to tease her about seeing her with Yash – for Christ's sake he was just a fun kid, a bit too big for his boots that's all! She had been dreading this – Hari, with his pious manner could put things in a way that could make it sound awfully perverted, she knew. Well, maybe he had got the message and would leave her alone henceforth. He bade them good night very gravely as a smiling Mathew chauffeured them back home later that night.

4

She remembered to take the fifteen rupees she owed the little boy, Sushant for the cowries before she set forth on her run the next morning. He had been watching out for her and came charging down the beach, grinning from ear to ear.

'Here you are,' she said, handing over the money and not breaking her stride.

'Thank you madam,' he said, pocketing the notes quickly and running alongside. 'Madam you live near to sea?' he asked.

'No,' she replied. 'I live in Delhi. No sea in Delhi, only a filthy river!'

'Ah, then madam, you need this.' And from the dirty canvas satchel flapping at his waist he produced a huge, craggy conch shell, ivory white, tinged with ochre and gold. 'With this you can hear sea anywhere,' he explained gleefully. 'Even in Delhi! Put to ear and listen! It has sea inside it forever!'

She grinned. 'I know, I know! You shouldn't pick all the shells from the seashore!'

'Not picking, getting caught in fishing net,' he said. 'You like?'

'It's beautiful,' she had to concede.

'Only forty rupees! Not even fifty! You can pay tomorrow. Day after also!'

'Ten!' she said automatically, and feeling the usual little pang of guilt.

They shook on the deal at twenty-five, and Maya went on her way. 'At this rate I'll be broke in a week,' she grinned, 'but will have quite a nice shell collection!'

On her return she spotted Smita and Asha on the beach as usual and spent a happy half hour playing with the toddler.

'You know, she's more gutsy than I am!' she told Smita. 'I'm petrified of getting out of my depth; yesterday I took quite a ducking! But just look at her! She plunges right in like a dolphin!'

'I know,' Smita agreed, 'sometimes she scares me blind! Regular little water baby she is!'

After another huge and magnificent breakfast, she was debating whether to ring Yash when the phone trilled.

'Darling Maya!' Sherry squealed happily. 'Get right over. The team has arrived!'

'The team?'

'For my shoot!'

'Oh, I thought that was for the evening…'

'Silly, but they still have to organize the shoot or whatever. We will be leaving for the location in an hour…'

'Location? I thought they'd shoot it here…'

'Darling, no! Daddy wouldn't hear of it. Said he wasn't having this place turned into some kind of commercial movie set. We're too exclusive for that darling! He wouldn't even allow them to shoot on the beach! But never mind, we've found a great location – actually it's on the beach where Billy's house is. So come along, we're leaving in an hour! See you!'

Slowly, Maya put the receiver down. She picked it up again and pressed the button for the Reception.

'Hi Yash, it's me Maya,' she said when the connection was made. 'Were you thinking of going to the rocks this morning?'

'Hi, yes, kind of thought we could build a huge fort and have fun attacking it!'

'Shit, I can't come. My cousin has lined up some kind of ad-film shoot and wants me to come along.' While a small hobgoblin voice piped up, 'so you'd rather build sandcastles with Yash than watch Sherry look beautiful in an ad film. What's wrong with you!'

'Do they want you to make up limericks for them?' Yash asked hopefully. 'You know like the one you made up about dirty Harry?'

She giggled. 'Idiot! Of course not!'

'Well, have a nice day!'

'Bye, I'll catch you later!'

She put down the receiver. 'Ma!' she called. 'I'll be spending the day with Sherry. Happy? Be back in the evening. Is that okay?'

Mrs Sabherwal emerged from her bedroom. 'Of course,' she said. 'We've come here so you can spend time with your cousins!'

She put on her new pair of pale peach shorts and a sleeveless T-shirt that confirmed, 'I'm a Peach!' and showed off her figure extra-nicely and walked down to the Sabherwal's villa. Four cars and a covered pick-up truck were parked outside along with a trailer-truck covered with tarpaulin. A dog handler and his helper were looking after half-a-dozen glossy Dobermans, with studded collars. There were people swarming all over the place, some eating out of paper plates, others slurping tea from saucers. On the veranda, Sherry was in animated conversation with a pony-tailed man with a goatee and rimless glasses, and another brawny looking guy, with slicked back hair and terrific biceps. Five more bodybuilder-types in black vests and jeans hung around, smoking.

'Ah Arunda and Donny – I want you to meet my cousin Maya. She'll be coming along for the shoot, if you don't mind… She's interested in seeing how ads are made, aren't you darling!' Sherry winked and raised her eyebrows.

'Sure, sure no problem!' Ponytail and Big Biceps grinned and waved casually at Maya who smiled shyly back. Who knew what might happen, she thought; imagine if they did ask her for a screen test after all!

'Come on guys, let's get rolling!' bellowed Arunda 'pack it in, let's go, let's go!'

Even so, it was a good hour before the convoy was ready to roll.

'So what's the ad about?' Maya asked Sherry as they bumped along in the car. 'And what's with the dogs?' Sherry was already looking earnestly into a hand-mirror her huge vanity case open on the seat beside her. She giggled.

'They're launching some big stud bike,' she said. 'But you're not supposed to tell anyone till the ad is out!'

'So you're just going to pose on it?' With your arms wrapped around Donny Big Biceps, but she didn't say that.

'No silly! There's a storyline. You see, I'm this mermaid who's stranded on this rock and being threatened by heavies and their dogs. Donny spots me and drives through hell and high water and rescues me!'

'A mermaid?'

Sherry giggled and shrugged. 'Idiotic isn't it! They just want to show that this bike can go just about anywhere. You know, up and down sand dunes, in the sea, over rocks and so on.'

They got to the location at last, a small, rocky, almost deserted beach about thirty minutes away from Shanbagh Resort. A recce team had surveyed the place before, but shooting angles and finetuning were still being finalized. It was well past noon when they began the shoot in earnest. First they drove back on the road and took long shots of Donny (the hero) banking stylishly along the coast road on a royal purple bike, stopping from time to scan the ocean (for stranded mermaids obviously, Maya thought with a giggle). Then, at last he spotted one! He stiffened. Down there, on a jagged rock, far out (and reminding Maya of her own Razor Rocks), Sherry sprawled stranded extravagantly as the five swarthy heavies surrounded her, urging their dogs on to the kill and preparing to fling their net around her. Sherry was clad in a skimpy green bikini top and the usual ridiculous mermaid's tail, which she flapped helplessly from side to side, making Maya giggle again. Hero Donny, (now replaced by a stuntman) roared off the cliff on his bike, and landed perfectly some ten feet below (the drop became a hundred feet in the final film) and then raced through the incoming breakers, sending the spray fountaining up from beneath his wheels, his engine growling gloriously. One by one he flattened the heavies, doing great wheelies and spraying sand in their faces and sending their Dobermans scampering away yelping, before riding his great bike right up the rocks to where the besieged mermaid lay, flapping her tail weakly. He took her in his arms and placed her sidesaddle (of course, her silly fishtail would get in the way) clinging on to him for dear life. And then she was there (in huge and glorious close-up in the film), hanging tight on to him, as he rode through miles of golden sea spray. She whispered something to him and he nodded briefly before turning the great bike straight into the sea and the sunset… and then rode back out again – without her. He gave one backward glance did one huge last wheelie (reminding Maya of those ancient Lone Ranger films) and was on his way…

Of course they had to do very many takes before everything was perfect and wrecked all the six bikes the company had supplied for the shoot by the end of it, but Sherry had been warmly congratulated, and hugged endlessly by virtually everyone for her performance. No one had ever had a mermaid with such a mass of haloed curls and sparkling eyes before, Arunda told her.

'You're going to become famous, my dear,' he promised. 'Just wait till they see this. The offers will come pouring in! And then we won't be able to afford you! I'm digging my own grave I tell you! You're the freshest face in ten years!'

And fluffhead or not Sherry had been true to her word. As they packed up at the end of the shoot, she buttonholed Arunda and asked, 'Do you think you could do a screen test for my cousin? She's very keen…' And followed it up with one of her pleading, spaniel looks.

Maya had seen him glance at her and alas, had also been within earshot of his reply.

'Not at the moment, my dear!' he told Sherry regretfully. 'She's a little too gaunt and broody. And we don't have an account for fairness creams or face powders at present!'

'They're too busy at the moment, darling,' Sherry had told her as they drove back. 'Maybe some time in the future! You have a lovely figure you know and great legs!'

'Thanks, Sherry,' Maya said. But her voice was smaller than she would have liked it to be.

It was approaching twilight as they drove back through the gates of Shanbagh Resorts, the sky still flame orange in the west, but mauve towards the east, and getting inkier by the minute. To their surprise, staff was scurrying through the trees, making for the edge of the cliff with torches and flashlights. Sherry sat up in the car and frowned.

'Oh my God, I hope some idiot hasn't gone and fallen over the edge!' she said. 'In spite of all those warning notices we have up! Driver stop!'

The two girls got off and ran towards the edge.

'Kya hua?' Sherry demanded in her boss's daughter voice.

'*Chokra phas gaya memsahib* – a little boy has got stuck, madam,' one of the staff replied.

They rushed to the edge of the cliff and peered over. Maya gasped and the blood drained out of her face. Clinging halfway up the sheer rocky cliff face was Yash, almost bleached by the lights being trained on him, both from above and below. But he didn't seem to be in the least bit afraid, or upset by his apparent predicament – just exasperated. One of the managers was dangling a rope down from the top close to him.

'Don't be afraid, son! Catch the rope and tie it around your waist,' he shouted. 'We'll pull you up!'

And peering down the cliff with his face glued to his camcorder was Hari, almost beside himself with excitement. Maya glanced around but Mr and Mrs Ahuja were nowhere to be seen.

'Mr Desai, what happened?' Sherry asked the manager who had lowered the rope.

He turned. 'One of the guests informed us that this little boy was stuck halfway up the cliff and was hurt. He was bleeding…'

'Oh my God! Yash are you all right?' Maya leaned over and yelled, feeling as if her own heart had just fallen off a cliff.

'Maya! Thank God! Will you tell these idiots to put off their lights – they're blinding me!' came Yash's exasperated voice from halfway down the cliff. 'There's enough light to climb up!' If he fell, Maya thought with a shudder, he's had it – there were rocks below, sharp razor rocks - not soft beach sand. And what was the idiot doing halfway up the cliff face anyway?

'My God, Maya, tell your midget boyfriend to hang on. If he'll fall…' Hari was beside her suddenly ghoulish in the glare of the emergency tubelights, and clearly hoping that the little boy would fall and be smashed on the rocks below. What live coverage that would be! He'd be on AXN in no time! Excitedly, he pointed his camera at Yash again and switched on a blindingly bright strobe light.

Maya clutched Sherry's arm. 'Sherry tell them to switch off the lights. He's getting confused and blinded!'

And so one by one the lights were turned off – excepting Hari's strobe that kept flashing on in short bursts. 'I have to cover this,' he repeated. 'It's my right! This is live news! Hard news! Oh wow!'

Then for about thirty seconds there were no lights on at all. Yash was right, there was still enough twilight to see by – though it was fading fast.

'Thanks,' he called up, sardonically. 'Now I can see where I'm going!' He looked up and began climbing up again and at that moment Hari switched on his strobe to catch the action. Blinded, Yash shielded his eyes with one hand and slipped precariously, hanging on with just one hand, his feet scrabbling for toeholds. And in one angry movement, Maya ripped the strobe out of Hari's grasp and flung it over the edge. It died slowly as it arced down and then smashed on the rocks below. Hari just opened and shut his mouth like a goldfish.

And she didn't hear what he muttered under his breath. 'Oh so it's like that is it?'

She was peering over the edge again, her heart hammering, as were the rest of the crowd, shouting encouragement. Yash had regained his equilibrium and had started making valiant progress up the rock face, swarming up it with the confidence of a monkey.

'He's a good climber,' one of the guests remarked. 'He knows exactly where to put his hands and feet.'

'Regular little chimpanzee!'

Within minutes his tousled head had appeared over the edge, and willing hands helped him over. He gazed with astonishment at the crowd.

'But what's….'

'Are you all right?' Maya had pushed through, her heart still thudding. 'Someone said you were hurt! Are you okay?'

Yash looked puzzled. Suddenly he held up his arm. Sure enough there was a cut near his elbow, which was trickling blood. 'Oh, you mean this? I must have scratched it some time, dunno. But why are…' He indicated at all the people – some who were beginning to drift away.

'Just come away from the edge and sit down here,' Maya said leading him to a bench and wondering why her own knees felt like buckling. 'Come on you silly goose, you scared everyone to death!'

'Son, what were you doing on the cliff? How did you get there?' Poor Mr Desai was beside himself with relief. If something had happened… Hari had belligerently thrust his way forward again with his camera.

'Yes, and can you tell our viewers how you got there in the first place?' he asked loudly.

Yash looked up at Hari and smeared a grubby palm over the camera lens. 'No comment,' he said, 'I don't talk to the press!' Hari gave a squawk of alarm and backed off, wiping his precious lens with a hanky. Yash looked at Maya and grinned.

'Madam lady!' he said hoarsely. 'A man needs a challenge! All day I have spent wandering on this beach kicking pebbles from one end to another and chasing crabs! Then I see the cliff and think, why take the steps when you can climb up directly? It will be a change!'

'A change! But you got stuck!'

'Did not. I just took a break on a ledge halfway up to admire the sunset,' the incorrigible boy replied, shrugging. 'Not my fault if everyone here panics and gets hysterical!'

Hari had thrust his face forward again. 'Do you know we almost fetched the fire brigade all the way from Chiplun? And by the way, where are your parents?' He was shouting almost, self-righteous and indignant, doing the boss's son act.

'Actually my parents have gone to this Chiplun place,' Yash said. 'They said they wanted to check out some ancient temples or something. I didn't want to go, so I stuck around.'

'Mr Yash, sir, please promise me that you'll never try anything like that again!' Poor Mr Desai had had a rough evening. 'Now come in to the lobby and have a soft drink with compliments of the management! And let's get some first aid on that arm.'

'Where's Papa gone?' Sherry asked him, wondering why her parents were not here.

'Oh, miss, your parents went to Chiplun too, with Mr and Mrs Ahuja. They should be returning soon. I tried to call them on their mobile, but there was no reply.'

'Well, all's well that's ends well,' Sherry remarked relieved as she played hostess in the coffee shop a few minutes later and ordered up magnum mango smoothies for them all. Hari had stomped off to playback his 'coverage' and see if it were good enough to show Mr Baga when he came next.

'You really are a little idiot!' Maya scolded after Sherry had gone, and feeling rather schoolmarmish. 'You do things without thinking of the consequences.' She also knew that she'd have to apologize to Hari tomorrow for smashing his strobe and offer to replace it. 'You know I threw Hari's strobe light over the cliff!' she went on. 'The creep just wouldn't turn it off. But really you shouldn't try such stunts!'

'I can't help it if everyone else is stupid!' Yash shrugged infuriatingly and then grinned. 'Say, that was cool!' And deepening his voice, 'Some good at least has come out of this misadventure! Next time you may throw his camera over!'

'Idiot! Just don't try it again!'

'So how was your day?' he asked. 'How was the great film shoot?'

Maya grinned. 'It was so funny,' she began but her smile faded away. *'A little too gaunt and broody and we don't have an account for a fairness cream or face powder...'*

Why had those words burned her so badly?

'Hey Maya, what's up? You got another limerick coming up?'

She shook her head, and smiled wanly.

'No such luck,' she said and got up to go. 'I'm tired now, I'll tell you about it tomorrow. Goodnight Yash, see you later.'

But later that night when she was in bed it came to her like a visit from the very devil, the second of the black and increasingly bitter limericks that would plague her that summer:

Maya thought she was a fairy queen
With a complexion all peaches and cream
But she was broody and gaunt
And all her fans she did haunt
Till they fled with dreadful screams!.

5

To her surprise, Yash was already out on the beach at five-fifteen the next morning when she set out for her run. He was lugging a huge black plastic bag behind him on a trolley. She stared at him and his baggage with astonishment.

'Hi! What's up?' she greeted him, smiling. 'What new heights are you planning to scale so early in the morning? Or are you fleeing after having broken into the hotel safe last night and cleaned out the guests' jewels? What's in that? Contraband? It looks heavy.'

He looked up and grinned delightedly. 'Hi Maya, I knew I could rendezvous with you here.' He indicated the bag. 'This has all our essentials and equipment for the day!'

'You want me to run away with you?' She snorted. 'We'll never get far dragging that behind us!' She smiled. 'But I'm flattered all the same!'

'No listen,' he said glancing at his ridiculous canary-yellow wristwatch. 'We got about three and a half hours to high tide, I checked.' He jerked a thumb in the direction of the rocks. 'So we gotta be there well before that!'

'What are you talking about?'

'We go out there to that cool cove at Razor Rock 3 and chill out,' he said simply. 'I got all the stuff we need here for a good time. Come on Maya, please!' Suddenly he was pleading, his big black eyes wide.

She sighed. 'Ummm I don't know,' she said doubtfully, but then knew that she did. 'Okay, but first I've got to go for my run! And then I'll have to inform my mom.' She frowned. 'Say but if the tide's coming in then we won't be able to get off that rock for at least five hours!'

He beamed mischievously. 'Exactly!'

She shook her head. 'I don't think my mom will be too pleased if I tell her, bye, I'm off to get stranded by the tide on a rock with a boy, see you in the afternoon! She thinks I should spend all my time with my cousins. Still I'll have a shot. After all I spent the whole day with Sherry yesterday!'

'Please come, Maya. Promise? It'll be really great!'

'Okay, this is how we'll do it. I'll go for my run, charge home and tell my mom. If she says yes, fine, I'll join you; if she's a dragon, well I'll run over and tell you anyway!' She pursed her lips and murmured, 'and maybe get caught there by the tide, who knows!'

He squinted at his watch again.

'Great! Don't be later than 0700 hours,' he instructed. 'See you!'

'Hey, you carrying stuff to eat and drink?' she asked.

'Oh the usual rations.' He brightened up. 'But you can bring what you want too!'

'Okay, I better be off!'

'You'll come, won't you?' he asked as she began jogging on the spot.

'Sure! Bye now, be seeing you!'

She was off and running, wondering what on earth the little hellion had been lugging in his sack and trolley and what he had planned for the day. She cut her run short by fifteen minutes and was back at the cottage by six-fifteen. To her dismay, her mother was still fast asleep, and she knew it would be foolish to awaken her. She was never in the best of tempers first thing in the morning. Ah, then, but this also provided the perfect solution to her problem. Smirking, Maya sat down at the dining table and wrote her note:

Dear Mom,

I'm off exploring with Yash Ahuja – the boy who came with us from Bombay. I'll be back well after lunch, so don't worry or wait up. We're not going anywhere too far, (she didn't want to specify exactly where of course, that would spoil the fun), and will always be within sight of the resort – promise! I've taken some stuff from the mini-fridge so we won't be hungry.

Love,

Maya

She propped it up prominently on the dining table and opened the mini-fridge. Mathew had kept it well-stocked – there were apples, mangoes, chickoos, as well as bread and buns and chocolate. In a cupboard she found a tin of sausages and mackerel and a small jar of olives (Pankaj Mama is really classy, she thought, if this is the sort of stuff he stocks for his guests). She took a couple of bottles of water, her sunscreen lotion and sunglasses and changed into her swimsuit. Grinning (and feeling like a thirteen year old playing hooky) she slipped out of the garden and down the steps. It was six-forty, so she had plenty of time. She glanced up and down the beach but to her relief it was deserted – even Smita had not shown up with Asha as yet, though she was due any minute. She clambered over the causeway ridge, and then ducking low, as if under fire, snaked her way towards Rock 1, grinning and wondering why the hell she was playing at commandos. She was being infected by Yash's idiotic ways! She clambered over Rock 2 and down again, noticing the tracks of Yash's trolley as well as his footprints. Poor guy, lugging that sack all by himself all this way! On either side of the causeway, the waves were swishing up vigorously, occasionally breaching the rocks and splashing over. In a short while, the sea would claim the causeway linking the Rocks, islanding them… Instinctively, Maya quickened her steps, a small faraway voice wondering if this was such a sensible idea after all…

She climbed up Rock 3; poor Yash must have had hell of a time hauling his trolley and sack up this. She walked across the top and then peered down over the edge at the sandy cove at the far end, keeping her head low, wanting to surprise Yash (and hoping he would be doing his Cannibal King item).

But it was she who was surprised. Astonished.

Yash was hard at work on the small sandy beach and had already constructed a large and very impressive fort – complete with crenellated battlements and flying buttresses and moat. His sack lay open beside him, and apart from the spades and buckets strewn around, a fleet of fifteen beautifully-made toy galleons and ancient sailing warships were arranged at the edge of the bay, next to a large foam exercise mat. As she watched, he pulled out a couple of plastic bags from his sack and emptied the contents on to the sand: battalions of gaily attired toy soldiers, musketeers with rifles at their shoulders, squinting down the barrels, commanders striking heroic poses on horseback, brandishing broadswords. And beautiful brass and iron cannons and guns, some on carriages, some not. These he arranged carefully on the battlements of the walls and the fort, before planting a standard on top of the main turret and assessed his handiwork, carefully smoothening out the sand and tidying up the landscape. Back he delved into his sack and emptied out another lot of colourful toy figurines, and much to her bewilderment, a couple of reels of thin twine. He picked up a ship and propped its masts upright – they had been folded down along the deck for storage she guessed. The sails too unfolded and suddenly there she was a miniature sailing ship in all her pristine glory. But just what on earth was the little imp up to? It was time to find out.

'Hi Yash, what on earth are you doing?'

He looked up slowly, a wide grin spreading across his face, his shock of hair sticking up.

'Hi Maya! You came! Oh, great! Come on down!'

She joined him. 'So what's with the fort and the armada?' she asked. She picked up a galleon and examined it. About twelve inches long it was made of wood and plastic beautifully detailed and crafted. She held it close and squinted. 'Hey, I can even read its name, "*HMS Victory*", and just look at these guns!' She frowned, 'wasn't that... wasn't that the name of....'

'Lord Nelson's ship!' he finished delightedly. 'And you see that gun on the deck? The stubby one with a snub nose? Its called a carronade – it could fire hundreds of musket balls at one shot and decimate the enemy.' He picked up another ship and held it up proudly. 'And this one's the *HMS Warrior* – Queen Victoria's warship. This is Captain Cook's ship, *The Endeavour*, and this one here is Blackbeard's ship, *Queen Anne's Revenge*! And this is the ship of Admiral Villeneuve, the *Bucentaure*. He led the French and Spanish fleet at the battle of Trafalgar.'

'Wow!' she said impressed. 'You know your history! You never cease to amaze me. And you have quite a VIP navy!' She frowned, 'But didn't most of these people live in different times?' she asked. 'Different centuries even?'

'Sure,' he said grinning. 'It doesn't matter – we're in charge now! We can change the course of history! We can do what we like!'

She was still examining the ships, picking them up one by one and looking at them closely. 'You know, some of these ships seem pretty battered. As if they've seen a lot of action on the high seas.' She was right, decks were cracked and chipped, the tiny wood panels obviously repaired, the hulls bore signs of impact and some of the masts had obviously snapped some time in the past. The sails, made of some canvas-like material, were neatly folded, and rolled down ingeniously to unfurl – some had been obviously patched up. But the repairs had been lovingly and painstakingly done. 'Do they float?' she asked, and set down the *HMS Victory* gently on the water. The great warship floated beautifully, riding the waves with aplomb, its sails flapping eagerly.

'Wow! That's cool! So what's with all this paraphernalia?' she asked.

'Come on, help me man the ships!' he said, handing a reel of twine. 'You have to tie these fellows to the masts like they are on leashes!'

'Tie... but why?'

'So that if they fall overboard during the battle they don't get lost! Even if the ship capsizes we can retrieve them. Just pull 'em out of the drink!'

'Oh... but what battle?'

'Here, come on!' He passed her a handful of figurines. Bemused she examined one.

'Yash,' she said grinning, and squatting back on her heels, 'I think you've given me the wrong lot. This fellow looks like a villainous pirate! Actually they're all pirates!'

'I know!' he said grinning back.

'You want to man Lord Nelson's and Queen Victoria's ships with *pirates*?' She snorted back a giggle. 'Isn't that being a little disrespectful?' She shook her head. 'Only you could distort history like that!'

He shrugged. 'It depends...' He rummaged a bit and pulled out several plastic Jolly Rogers. 'Here, plant these on top of the ships!'

'You really are quite something!'

'I know! Okay, now put the ships in the water, but first tether them to your legs or around your waist so they don't just float about anywhere.'

'To my legs...?'

'Because you're going to need your hands to fire your guns, silly!' He lowered his voice and spoke hoarsely. 'To fire that evil carronade!'

'Fire guns? What guns?' she asked helplessly.

'Silly we're going to fight a battle like I told you. That's a notorious pirate fleet that's terrorized the world and which is going to attack Fort Razor Rock for the gold buried in its dungeons.'

'What gold?' she couldn't help asking. 'I don't see any gold!'

He dug around busily at the base of the main turret of Fort Razor Rock. And to her amazement unearthed a small wooden chest, crammed with gold-wrapped chocolate coins. 'Pieces of eight! Gold sovereigns!' he said, shutting the chest firmly and burying it again.

'You… you actually brought that over and buried it here for the game?' The fellow produced one amazing surprise after another.

'It's no fun otherwise,' he pointed out simply. 'You've got to fight for *something*! Now do you want to be the bloodthirsty scallywags or the brave defenders of Fort Razor Rock? I'll let you have first choice because it's the first time you're playing!' He glanced at her. 'You will play won't you?' he asked.

I'm seventeen, she thought, seventeen! And I'm about to start playing war games and treasure hunts with this crazy little fellow, I must be nuts! She nodded. 'Sure,' she said. 'Okay, so I'll be the terrible Pirate Queen of the High Seas, and my command ship is *The Warrior*, which I've taken on charter from Queen Victoria!' She giggled as Yash looked thrilled. 'Okay, so how do I attack the fort?' she asked.

'With this,' he said, delving into his sack again and producing a catapult and a bag of ball bearings, some of which were pretty large. 'You bring your ships as close as you dare and open fire with your cannons at the fort, trying to destroy it.' He pointed out to a small turret in the middle of the fort, surrounded by high walls and bristling with musketeers and cannons. 'That's the ammo dump. Hit it and you destroy the fort and can loot the gold,' he grinned, 'if you can!' he added. The clever little imp had located the ammo dump so cunningly it would take a very lucky shot to hit it, surrounded as it was by a phalanx of high walls and towers.

'And what do you do?' she asked, flexing the catapult experimentally.

'Try to sink your ships of course,' he said simply.

'With your own catapult or with mine?' She grinned. 'If you want mine, you'll have to be nice to me, and it'll be the first time in military history that both sides share the same weapons during a battle.'

'No,' he said, 'I use these!' He cupped his hands around a fistful of wet sand and produced a tennis ball sized cannonball. 'I lob these at your ships!'

For a moment she was shocked. 'But won't they damage and even wreck those beautiful ships?' she asked.

He shook his head. 'Not really! Sometimes a mast gets cracked or snaps and the rigging and sails become a mess, but that's about all.' He grinned, 'but because they're so heavy they can sink or capsize a ship so you better watch out.' And added with a sigh, 'Actually I would have loved using the ball bearings – they're more like real cannonballs, but those can really smash the ships up and hole them and then repairing them is a pain and takes ages.'

'Hey, wait a minute! It's not fair. You have all the big firepower – those aren't cannonballs, those are bombs! And I just have these puny ball bearings which will bury themselves in the walls of the fort and have no impact at all.'

'Oh, well all right!' He glanced at her slyly and delved back into the bottomless pit that was his sack. 'Here,' he said, 'you can also use these!' And extracted a carton of old tennis balls and six medium-sized coconut shells. 'Your big guns! Your heavy weapons!'

'You must be nuts!' she said, her grave eyes widening. 'You've been lugging all this junk around just for this game? You really are a war game fanatic!'

'It's fun Maya,' he said simply. 'Come on, give it a shot!'

'Okay!' she grinned, wading forth into the water with her fleet. 'Heck, I feel like Gulliver's wife! To arms! The Pirate Queen of the High Seas prepares to attack! Surrender or die, little dog!'

Yash whooped and hunkered down by his fort. 'You get the first shot you mangy wench! You're attacking!'

'Mangy wench, eh! Take that!' She put a ball bearing into her catapult and drew bead. 'Hey, little Cannibal King,' she called, 'stand aside. I'm not too sure of my aim and wouldn't want to disable you personally!'

Quickly he scampered aside and she let fly. The ball bearing hit a turret, scattering a couple of musketeers and dislodging a cannon, but did no major damage.

'Ho-ho madam, you'll have to do better than that!' He tossed a cannonball up and Maya watched as it curved high and then began to fall. With a gentle tug she moved her ships out of the way and it splashed down harmlessly.

'Hey! You can't do that!'

'Can too! That's just evasive action! Now stand aside, I'm opening up with my big guns! Surrender the treasure or prepare for annihilation!' She drew bead with one of the coconuts and flung it at the fort with all her might. So hard that she lost her balance and fell flat into the water with a scream, taking *The Endeavour*, *The Golden Hinde* and *The Bounty* down with her.

'Ho-ho-ho-ho!' Yash rolled on the sand with laughter. 'Madam Pirate Queen is sinking her own ships! Talk about friendly fire!'

She rose spluttering, wiping her eyes and laughing. She pointed to his fort. 'I lost three ships maybe, but look at your fort buster! Your flag is down and your commander has fallen off his horse and is lying upside down in the mud! Surrender or die!'

The coconut had smashed straight into the main turret of the fort, wrecking it completely. The flag that Yash had stuck on the top lay forlornly on one side and the commanding officer lay half-buried in the sand, musketeers scattered around him.

'Surrender? Never!' yelled Yash, and lobbed two cannonballs simultaneously. One scored a direct hit on *The Victory* making her stagger and list alarmingly, the second landed on the back of Maya's neck. She squealed.

'Sorry!' he yelled. 'I didn't mean that. You came in the way!'

Grinning, she picked up a tennis ball and drew bead on him. Laughing he scampered away and she let it fly once more at his fort. And then let loose a fusillade, with the other balls and coconut shells before he could retaliate.

'Hey, that's not fair!' he shouted, dancing up to the water's edge and keeping an eye on the ball she still had in her hand. 'It's my turn to fire!'

'All's fair in love and war, little villain!' she yelled gleefully. His fort had taken several terrible hits and was looking extremely battered. The walls and towers surrounding the ammo dump had crumbled and it was helplessly exposed. Another good shot… She was about waist deep in the water, when she felt the urgent swell nudge and splash against her back. Her surviving ships floated shorewards briskly, and suddenly there was water slopping into the moat around Yash's fort. She turned around, surprised. The swells were racing into the cove, one behind the other in quick succession.

'Hey Yash, I think we need to call a truce! It looks like the tide's coming in!' she called as another wave came sloshing in at speed. 'We'd better gather up our armies and get up on the rocks. There's a convenient ledge about halfway up where we can bivouac. I don't know how much of the beach gets flooded!' Quickly she began gathering up her fleet and its bedraggled crew as he picked up his musketeers and cannons from the battered fort. They stuffed them back into the sack, and grinning slyly she quickly dug up the buried 'treasure' and smuggled it into the capacious pocket of her towelling robe, while he was busy putting his ships away. They retreated up the rocks, dragging the loaded trolley behind them. It wasn't too difficult getting up to the sandy ledge halfway up and they dumped their stuff there and sat down.

'Let's unroll the exercise mat and be really comfy,' Maya suggested, which is exactly what they did. A few minutes later, she looked down at the cove and giggled.

'Oh my Cannibal King, surrender or drown!' she intoned. 'Your fort is being taken by the sea on my command for I am Pirate Queen of the High Seas!'

'I will drown rather than surrender to a siren of the sea. Glub-blub-blub-blub!' He rolled his eyes and lay back, writhing and coughing.

'And sir, you have forgotten to dig up your gold!'

'Oh, shit!' he exclaimed and peered over the ledge. 'It's too late – the sea's taken it!'

'Too bad, eh?' she said. 'Now let's have something to eat!'

'Give me the kiss of life, oh Pirate Queen,' he gasped. 'And maybe I won't have you for lunch!'

'Hmm... I think you'd prefer these,' she said producing the treasure chest. His eyes bulged.

'You... you looted the fort!' he gasped.

'It was my duty!' she replied gravely. 'I am the Pirate Queen after all!' And added generously, 'but I'll share the loot with you only because I did it while you were taking care of my ships.'

He shook his head in dismay. 'You'll never make it as a Pirate Queen with that attitude,' he pointed out glumly.

'And you really are an idiot you know. Now can you open this tin?'

They picnicked happily on their sandy ledge, sharing their loot (melting rapidly now) and watching the sea swirl and suck hungrily below them. The little silver beach had been completely flooded and Maya watched hawk-eyed as the water level below rose. She knew they were in absolutely no danger – they could always climb higher if the water came up, but she didn't think it would. She was right – it filled the cove, lapping the rocky walls to a height of about three or four feet at the most.

'Lady!' Yash said suddenly, rolling his eyes and staring at her fixedly. 'We're stranded on this rock! I must warn you again, I might have to kill you and eat you! For I am the Cannibal King!'

She grinned at him. 'You say some of the most idiotic things, you know!' she said.

He picked out three sausages from the tin, and began working on them with his penknife, cutting off bits and using the snazzy little plastic toothpicks that had come with the tin (it was a very classy tin) muttering under his breath as he did. Then, proudly he held out the human figure he had made out of them, the face nicely carved, the mouth with a grimace of terror stretched across it, the arms obviously bound behind the back.

He fixed her with a basilisk look. 'Oh Siren Queen of the Pirates! I have brought a human sacrifice for you! If you are truly worthy to rule the seas, you will cut his head off and devour him raw!'

'He'd look and taste a lot better if you empty that sachet of ketchup over him first,' she replied tartly, grinning. 'Besides, you're the cannibal, remember?'

His eyes popped.

'And don't try to gross me out so you can scoff the lot!'

'Oh! I wasn't!' But he glanced up at her with a sheepish grin.

'You are an idiot you know,' she said and added severely, 'and stop trying to look down the top of my swimsuit all the time!'

'It is my duty!' he responded with dignity. 'I would be failing in my duty if I didn't!'

'Idiot. You talk a lot of rubbish!'

'It's been said before.'

'Not surprising! So which grade are you in?'

'Does it matter. Provided I learn the right things! What about you?'

'I was supposed to appear for my boards, but wasn't allowed to!'

'Oh, and why was that?'

'Um…because…well I didn't study enough they said! Didn't do well enough in the pre-boards. You got any brothers and sisters?'

'Nope, I'm an only the lonely! What about you?'

'A younger brother.'

'Oh yep – you mentioned him. The genius!'

'Well he can't help that!' She sighed.

'Bet it doesn't help you too much!'

'Sometimes.'

'Is that why you make up those cool limericks?'

'I don't know. They just come.' She shrugged. 'Especially when things happen or I'm upset!'

'Can you make up one now?'

'Nope. If I try – they just don't come. They just pop up readymade like!'

'Wish I could do that! It's a tragedy! I know so many people I could make limericks about!'

'It's a gift!'

'I suppose! You're lucky! You know what?'

'What?'

'We haven't checked out that little rock at the side!'

'We'll have to wait till the tide goes out. There's thirty feet of sea sloshing between it and us!'

'Say you know the owner of this resort pretty well!'

'Sure, I told you he's my uncle. My ma's brother!'

'Oh yup! Sorry, I forgot! Oh yes, and the lout and the squealer are your cousins! You must have fun!'

'Well Hari is a creep, but Sherry's not so bad. Bit of an airhead.' She swallowed. 'They think they're trying to help me – you know give me a leg up!'

'Up where?' He glanced at her long bronzed limbs. 'They look very strong. Like pythons actually.'

'Thank you! They think I'm dumb. You know, I bombed this year and have always come in the bottom three in class…'

'You're not dumb. You're fun!'

'Thanks!'

'Bet none of them can make up those cool limericks! I can't!'

'Of course you can't! I told you it's a gift!'

'What's the thing that scares you the most?'

'Scares me the most? Um…at the moment it is finding myself in the sea without being able to touch the ground! It happened to me yesterday and I freaked! I get nightmares about that. What scares you the most?'

'Climbing up cliff faces at twilight!'

'Big deal! Come on, what really scares you?'

'Um well, can't think of anything!'

'Liar! Oh, by the way I meant to ask you. My cousins are throwing a beach party tomorrow night. You're invited.'

'Actually that's what I'm most scared of!'

'Please come. I have to go! I'd die of boredom alone!'

He stood up and bowed sweepingly before her. 'A damsel in distress eh? Do I hear a damsel in distress? Yes, and gallantly I shall come along to your rescue.' He clicked his tongue reprovingly. 'Alas, I can never resist a damsel in distress. It shall be my downfall one day but of it is so fated, so be it!'

'You talk too much nonsense. But thanks!'

'But you'll owe me big!'

'Sure! Anything you say!'

He grinned cheekily. 'Even a peek down your swimsuit?'

'I'll take your trunks off and throw them into the sea and spank you in a minute, Mr Half Pint, if you don't watch what you say!'

'Be my guest! Don't blame me when you swoon when you see the dragons on my bum! Ferocious flamethrowers, every one of them!'

'Ass. You really are an ass!' But she couldn't help giggling.

'You must have loads of friends,' he said enviously. Anyone who could make up limericks on the spot must have loads of friends. Fans even.

'Not really! Most of the kids I hang out with think I'm weird. And anyway all my classmates have gone ahead now.'

'Oh! Too bad! I thought people would be asking for your autograph!'

'Big deal!' She smiled, 'but I can give it to you if you want! And how about you? Girls hanging on every arm lapping up your nonsense I suppose?'

'Every time I find someone I can talk to for ten minutes without getting bored, we leave for another city,' he said shrugging. 'Most of the kids I've hung out with think we're running from the cops!'

'Too bad, huh?'

'Not as bad as having friends who don't like limericks! Sheesh! They must be jerks!'

'So what does you dad do that makes you travel so much?'

'He's some computer troubleshooting wizbang. His firm keeps shunting him around all over the world and we have to tag along.'

'So you must be mad about computers and computer games!'

He nodded. 'I like them, but sometimes I like real games better. Like the one we played just now. You don't play those by yourself! And you play with real things!'

She grinned. 'Well it was fun!' she admitted. 'I haven't had fun like that for ages!'

'So we can play it again tomorrow?'

'Hmm… we'll see!'

'So what does your dad do?'

'He's some hotshot in a big firm that makes machines for car factories or something.'

'Oh.'

'How old are you?' she asked.

'Eighteen… will be nineteen soon!'

'Sure. And you drive a Ferrari I suppose.'

'Test drive…'

'Of course, sorry!'

'Okay, then seventeen!'

'Eleven!'

'No way! I'll be fifteen soon!'

'Ah! Wow! The truth at last!'

'And you?'

'None of your business, buster!'

'Big deal! That's not fair! Twenty-five?'

'Rubbish! I'm not so decrepit!'

'Twenty-five then? No? Thirty? Do I hear thirty? From the lady in the green swimsuit? Going, going…'

'Idiot!' she said dissolving into fits of giggles. 'I'm seventeen!'

'Wow! A real spring chicken, eh?'

'Yash, you talk too much nonsense!'

'It's been mentioned before. So where do you live?'

'In Delhi.'

'Is it nice?'

'Not as nice as here!'

Of course! We might come to Delhi too!'

'On a holiday?'

'To live! My dad wants to set up his own firm!'

'That would be great!'

'What's it like?'

'Hot! But there are a lot of historical buildings and new shopping malls and the Metro and stuff!'

He looked thoughtful. 'Anything else so I can sell the place to my parents?'

'You'd like to live there?'

'Well, it would be the first time I'd have a readymade friend in a place we move to.'

'Sometimes you can be quite sweet you know.'

'Charming, actually!'

'Sure. Sorry!'

He yawned suddenly, and she caught it. 'Mmm… I think I'm going to have a snooze!' he announced and lay down. There was more than enough space for both of them to spread out in comfort, and the ledge was cool and in shadow. She watched him settle down. He was out like a light within minutes curled up his face turned towards the mossy rock face, his ribs rising and falling steadily. She felt a faint prickle on her shoulders and glanced at them, they were dusky golden brown and glossy. Better put on some more sunscreen lotion she thought, slipping her swimsuit straps free of her arms and unscrewing the tube. She applied the lotion and suddenly drowsy herself, lay down and closed her eyes...

She awoke with a start not knowing how much later. The sun had slipped around and was slanting down strongly straight into her eyes. Blinking she sat up, wondering for a moment where on earth she was and then remembering. Oh, shit just what was the time! They'd be throwing a fit at the resort… Nearby Yash lay sprawled flat on his back fast asleep his arms spreadeagled, his eyelashes fluttering. His sturdy looking chest, just with a hint of golden down on it, rose and fell rhythmically and he had a very cute belly button indeed. He still had his ridiculous canary yellow watch strapped to his wrist. Quietly, Maya knelt over him and reached for it. It swivelled round easily and she saw to her relief that it was just 2 o'clock. No need to panic and the tide would be nicely out now and she'd told her mother that she wouldn't be back for lunch. She glanced back at Yash's face and saw that his eyes were open now, wide and round. He was staring stunned at her warm brown breasts, now swinging completely free of her swimsuit, (whose straps she had stupidly forgotten to hitch back over her shoulders) just inches from his face. Both of her chocolate brown nipples were exposed, and as she silently mouthed 'oops!' and shifted back one of them brushed gently against his cheek.

For once he said nothing, 'just looked thunderstruck, wonderstruck and awestruck' she told herself later on, with the hint of a crooked smile. And had given a little gasp. And strangely she hadn't minded his looking or been embarrassed.

'It was just a wardrobe malfunction!' she repeated to herself and to explain it away. Which, of course it was... while another evil little voice piped up gleefully, 'And not a Freudian slip, miss?' And it was just the little bugger's luck that he had opened his eyes at that moment. Amazingly he had had the good sense – for once – not to embarrass her. She had drawn back slowly, adjusted her costume and said calmly:

'Come on, Yash, it's time we went back. They'll kick up a fuss otherwise.'

He got up, dusted his hands on his trunks nonchalantly and looked down at the cove.

'Will you look at that!' he said, whistling low. 'It's like brand new again!'

She looked down. He was right. The sandy cove was calm and pristine as it had been the first time she had been here. The sand was smooth and silvery, and delicately ribbed, spangled with a few stranded starfish and dark green mussels.

'Let's go for a dip,' she decided suddenly. 'I'm all hot and sweaty. It'll cool us down and we can go back afterwards.'

'Last one into the water is a hippo with a toothache!' he yelled leaping down.

From the top of the rock, Hari smirked and settled down with his camcorder.

As soon as the tide had withdrawn far back enough to expose the causeway, he had set out for the rocks. He had reached Razor Rock 3, and peered over its top down at the cove, but had seen no one there. At the time, Maya and Yash had been fast asleep on their ledge, which fortunately for them, was completely concealed from the top by its deep overhang ('like a parapet' Maya had said.). Puzzled, Hari had wandered about at a loss then tracked back to Razor Rock 2, which was also deserted. He returned to Rock 3, but first explored Little Rock, now accessible through just knee-deep water. There was a tricky jumble of rocks to be negotiated before you climbed onto it proper – you had to feel your way very carefully because some of them wobbled unpleasantly when you stepped on them. Also the sand had been scooped deeply from the base of Little Rock by surging tidal currents. He could see the watermark left by the retreating tide, a good three feet above his head. But there were convenient step-like rocks by which you could get on to the rock – and enter a small sandy alcove well above the watermark. That was pretty much all that there was to Little Rock. No Maya and midget boyfriend here either, (how he would have relished that!) but it was extremely interesting nevertheless. He decided to give Razor Rock 3 one last check – and peered over the edge just in time to see midget boyfriend leap into the water, followed by Maya.

Much to his disappointment he got no sensational coverage, and nothing that could be misconstrued or thought improper, nothing of interest to the paparazzi. Maya and Yash just swam and messed about in the water, as any normal kids would do, not even whooping too much. He shut his eyes and told himself, 'Be patient! Your time will come. Just keep at it!'

And for most of the time, he focused closely on Maya as his nose leaked slowly and he wiped it from time to time with the back of his hand.

'Come on now,' Maya said at last, pushing her sparkling hair away from her face. 'We'd better get back. We better collect all the stuff we left up on the ledge. Yash shook his head.

'Let's just leave it there. We'll come back tomorrow for another game!'

'Okay,' she agreed shrugging. 'They're your toys! You sure you want to leave your lovely ships here overnight?'

'Don't worry,' he said. 'Nothing will happen to them. No one knows about this place but us. And think, then we won't have to lug it all the way here tomorrow.'

Hari ducked low behind cover as they came up to the top of the rock and then descended. He waited until they were well down the causeway and then went up to the ledge. He rummaged in the bag and looked in puzzlement at the ships he pulled out one by one. 'God help us, she's playing with his toys now!' he muttered, little realizing he had hit the bull's-eye. 'This will really be worth following up!'

Back at the cottage there was hell to chew as her mother railed her out. 'Again you disappear for the whole day Maya! Poor Sherry has come three times to look for you. She wanted to show you the shopping arcade! Really, you have no consideration!'

'Ma, I wrote in my note where I was going and when I'd be back! I can't help it if you were sleeping! I didn't want to disturb you!'

'Thanks for your concern. But what will Sherry darling and Hari *beta*, think, eh? Their cousin comes down from Delhi and disappears for the whole day, every day!'

'Ma, I really much prefer the company of Yash. He's fun! He's really so wacky!'

'And loafing about with a boy half your size! Really Maya, have some sense! Grow up! You're seventeen and behave like you're seven! Running around with children! In three-four years you'll be getting married even! And look at you, like a darkie already!'

Somehow she escaped the shrill harangue and it was a little later that evening that the dreadful thought struck her. Neither she nor Yash had said a word about the incident at the ledge… but for God's sake he could quite justifiably think that she had been trying to seduce him or something – while he slept! She buttonholed him at the first available opportunity – in the table tennis room that evening.

'Come on, I have to talk to you,' she said firmly, taking his arm.

'Okay, okay, I'm coming!' He glanced askance at her.

'What… what happened on the ledge… you know… was an accident! I was just checking the time. I'd put on more suntan lotion and went to sleep forgetting to hitch my swimsuit straps up again. Then I woke and panicked about the time… I'm sorry if I… er surprised you…,' she ended lamely with a rather weak smile.

He held up his hand as if blessing her. 'Go in peace, dusky maiden go in peace!' he said hoarsely grinning wickedly. 'Your secret is safe with the Cannibal King! And may he always be at your side when more such accidents happen! For whosoever sees the Pirate Queen with her….'

'Shut up! Idiot! You talk too much rubbish! There won't be any more such accidents, you can bet your fat fanny on that!'

6

'You're not to disappear today,' Mrs Sabherwal ordered Maya after she had returned from her run the following morning. There had been no sign of Yash on the beach though Smita and Asha as usual had been playing in the water – a little farther out than usual – because the tide was still quite far out. 'Go and spend time with Hari and Sherry.'

Maya made a face. 'They'd probably still be sleeping,' she said. 'They like sleeping late.'

'Then wait till they wake up,' her mother said exasperatingly, as Maya stared at the Razor Rocks.

It was smiling Mathew who came to her rescue again. 'Sherry miss has said that she is spending day at Billy's sahib's house to organize party for tonight. Hari sir is very excited because the *Instantnews!* TV team has arrived,' he said.

'See Ma, they're busy!'

'And what did I tell you?' Mrs Sabherwal raised an eyebrow. 'Of course they're awake and busy. Go – they're probably thinking you are sleeping.'

'Ma, they know I go for a run every morning,' Maya said, examining the neat scallop shells she had been given by Sushant ('complimentary madam – you are my best customer!') that morning.

'Just go, Maya. It looks so bad – we have been here three-four days and you haven't spent any time with your cousins!'

'Oh, okay,' Maya said ungraciously, getting to her feet. 'You forget I went modelling with Sherry for a whole day!'

She was walking slowly through the coconut groves towards the Shanbagh's villa, dragging her feet like a schoolgirl on the way to the principal's office when Yash appeared suddenly by her side.

'Hi,' he said eagerly. 'Coming to the Rock?'

She made a face and shook her head. 'I'll try but I don't think so. My mom wants me to spend the day with my cousins.'

'Oh,' he said shrugging. 'Well okay, then another time!' And added darkly, 'If there is another time…' He gestured eloquently.

'What do you mean?' she asked, stopping.

'We're leaving for Goa tomorrow,' he said simply. 'I thought it would be fun to have another battle on the rock! I mean the navy's still docked there!'

'Oh,' she said nonplussed and dragging her feet even more as she began to walk again. 'Okay, I'll try to get away – but can't promise.'

But luck was on her side. A media van (with *'Instantnews!'* emblazoned in electric blue along its sides) was parked outside and in the veranda Hari was in earnest conversation with a pretty young woman. Then Sherry came out of the house, followed by four men staggering under the weight of two big cardboard boxes. They loaded the boxes into one of the resort's pickup trucks parked in the driveway.

'Maya, darling, where were you all of yesterday?' Sherry tinkled, as Hari shot her angry looks.

'Oh, just messing around. What's going on?'

'Darling, I'm just off to Billy's place for the day to organize the do! You know, left to himself he's hopeless. He'll forget something vital and then go running around at the last minute like a headless chicken… But I'll be back by the evening and we'll leave together at about eight. How does that sound?'

'Oh,' she said as Sherry went on breathlessly and without pausing.

'I would love to have you along – but we're the hosts and you're the guest of honour and I'm not the daughter of a hotelier for nothing, not to know the difference between the two.'

'Oh,' said Maya and looked towards Hari who was going purple in the face trying to hush Sherry. Sherry glanced at him and giggled. 'Oh, and Hari's also very busy today – he's going to escort these poor *Instantnews!* chicks around, and getting interviewed and feeling important! Just today darling you'll have to amuse yourself till the evening – we'll make it up to you later, promise.' She fixed her big pleading eyes on Maya.

'No problem,' Maya said her heart suddenly light. 'I'll be fine. Really I will! Okay, bye then, Sherry, see you in the evening!'

'Love you, darling! Have a nice day!'

Hari watched her go for a moment before turning back to pretty Ruchika Sharma of *Instantnews!* No way he'd be able to follow Maya around today – he had more important things on the agenda – but well there was always tomorrow and the day after. Maya was here for quite a while and he could bide his time.

Back through the groves Maya walked, her steps light and brisk.

'Ma, both Sherry and Hari are busy today…,' she called through the bathroom door, back at the cottage.

'It serves you right!' Mrs Sabherwal called back, 'for ignoring them for all this time. Did you think they were going to wait hand and foot on you?'

'So I'm off to the beach. I'll be back usual time, and don't worry – I'm not going swimming in the sea. You know how scared I am of the water.'

'Will you be back for lunch?'

'No, I'll pack something! It's too much of a hassle to come back and then go out again. Bye Ma!'

She shut the bedroom door firmly, so she wouldn't hear anything further, raided the mini-fridge and was out of the gate three minutes later. She sped down the beach and on to the causeway, and then slowed up, wondering why she was in such a hurry. High tide was not for another hour and a half at least, but well, she had to have enough time in hand to get back if Yash were not at Rock 3. She climbed up it and hastened across, ducked down behind a rock and peered down into the little cove.

He was there of course, and a soft smile broke out as she saw his sturdy figure wade up and down through the shallows, trying to organize his navies. By the looks of it he was getting extremely frustrated with his armada, which he had divided into two, seven ships on one side and eight on another, broadside to each other ready for battle and kept shaking his head with exasperation. Probably he had not tethered them properly and they infuriatingly bobbed away or circled round and round on the gentle swells. Actually you really did need two people to fight the kind of battle he was trying to, and up on her ledge Maya's smile widened and she felt her cheeks suddenly warm. He'd thrown caution to the winds and was using the catapult as his weapon of choice, but with round sea pebbles as his ammunition. He'd stand alongside one flotilla of ships and aim his catapult at the other, fire his shot, then wade across to the other navy and fire back. But it was clear that the battle was not going according to plan. The *HMS Victory* had turned her prow towards Africa, plainly unimpressed, *The Bounty* had already foundered on the beach *The Golden Hinde* was scudding away as fast as she could go and *The Endeavour* and *Queen Anne's Revenge* had rammed each other. Maya grinned and slipped down the rocks to the beach.

'Hi, Yash! I think you need a Pirate Queen to show you how sea battles are fought!' she called softly, putting her hands on her hips. 'What do you think?'

He turned and stared at her a slow smile of sheer delight lighting up his face. It was so wonderful to be able to make someone smile like that Maya thought, her cheeks flushing suddenly. Yash smiled because he was just plain happy, happy to see her. And that made it even more wonderful. He nodded, suddenly serious.

'Ah, so the evil Pirate Queen and Siren of the Seas, returns to plague these waters! My armada awaits to send her leaking tubs to the blackest depths!'

'Flee now or walk the plank, vile knave!' she said tossing back her head and stifling her giggles with difficulty.

'Okay,' he said. 'Come on into the water. You take command of those eight ships there!' He pushed eight warships towards her and tossed her a reel of twine.

'Ah!' she said, picking up a ship and reading its name, 'and as I have just beheaded that blackguard Blackbeard I shall commandeer his warship, *Queen Anne's Revenge*!

'A straight sea battle it shall be then, madam. Seven versus eight on the high seas!' He grinned and winked and added *sotto voce*, 'And as you are a lady you shall get the first shot!' He squinted at the ships, puckered his brow and nodded slowly, a smile of evil glee breaking out. 'Say, I just got a better idea; should we replicate the battle of Trafalgar?' he suggested. 'I mean to the extent possible with just fifteen ships.'

'And how would we do that?' she asked wondering what he was now up to.

'Right,' he said, 'you take command of *The Victory* there and those six more ships and make them sail in single file in two lines, like this.' Quickly he sketched on the sand, what he meant. 'And I'll be Admiral Villeneuve commanding the *Becentaure* and arrange my ships like so.'

'It's like a reversed Euro symbol,' Maya said frowning, 'you're the curving bow shaped part and I'm the stalks.'

'Whatever!' he shrugged, 'it's how the battle was fought, Nelson sort of used his fleet like a battering ram.'

'Ah, vile knave and I presume you know who won the battle of Trafalgar, don't you?' she declared, 'prepare for annihilation.'

'You presume too much, madam Siren of the Seas! Prepare for history to be rewritten,' he replied, and added wistfully, 'I wish we had more ships. This will be such a puny battle!'

'Doesn't matter! Come on! I want to open fire with my carronade!'

'Here,' he said, handing her a catapult and a fistful of pebbles. 'Do your worst!'

'You want to use these?' she asked doubtfully. 'You'll wreck your beautiful ships!'

He nodded, his eyes sparkling recklessly. 'Yes. Let's make this as real as we can! I can always fix the ships afterwards! Fire evil Siren Queen!'

'Right buster!' She took aim and stretched the rubber back. The catapult slipped and took off like a wounded bird, landing with a plop in the water. 'Oh, damn!'

'Lord Nelson would have been very annoyed!' he hooted. 'My turn to fire!' Gleefully he yanked back his catapult to the maximum aiming carefully. His heavy calibre pebble smashed hard into the side of *The Victory* just above the water line and Maya winced as she heard the wood splinter and crack. *The Victory* was holed! 'Anyone who scores a direct hit gets a free second shot!' he yelled gleefully, yanking back the catapult again. He fired and scored another direct hit on the stricken ship, very close to and just below the first. She was taking in water rapidly, and listing alarmingly.

'Hey buster! You can't make up the rules of engagement as you go along!'

Whizz crack crunch! The ship shuddered again under the third impact and slowly keeled over.

'Dine with the fishes, scallywags, dine with the fishes! I'm rewriting history here man, rewriting history!'

'You can't change the course of history just like that, vile knave,' she yelled, 'and don't say I didn't warn you! I am the Siren Queen of the waves and have great powers of the ocean at my command!' She jumped up with her legs folded beneath her and landed in the water with a tremendous splash, sending a tidal wave speeding towards his fleet, broadside on.

'You have awoken the Siren of the High Seas with that silly peashooter of yours!' she declaimed laughing, and getting back to her feet. 'Now pay the price for you foolishness, little man!'

Five of his eight ships had capsized due to the wave, (so had four of hers) and the remaining three had been beached on the shore. He had been routed! He stared horrified at his capsized and beached fleet and then into her grave dark eyes, and laughing face.

'Eeeagh! Vile sea witch! You are but a Siren of the Seas! I am the Dragon of the Deep! Be gone!' He charged towards her splashing water into her face, and landed flat on his tummy beside her as she laughed and dodged. For a moment he floated in the clear shallow water, his arms extended over his head, looking at her sideways with sparkling eyes.

Maya shook the water from her face and stared at his lean brown shoulders and back.

'Surrender little Dragon of the Deep!' she hissed bending over him. 'I have you at my mercy!' And added tenderly, wolfishly, 'And do you know what Siren Queens do to their victims my Dragon of the Deep? This!'

And gracefully but deftly, slipped his bright red trunks right off and cast them aside. His bottom was brown and bare, a shade paler than his back and shoulders.

'Hey mighty admiral, your bottom is bare! Your flame-throwing dragons have fled! Surrender! But may I have the pleasure of a pinch?' He struggled to his feet, spluttering and gasping, his little brown penis penduluming indignantly as he tried to regain his balance.

'Yikes!' he yelped looking down at himself and realizing that his defenses were down and the cause was lost. 'Oh bloody hell!' Then he looked up at her slowly, a shy smile of surrender breaking out; she was watching him, pursing her lips, holding down a giggle, a strange shimmering light reflecting from her eyes. His Adam's apple bobbed as he struggled to recover.

'Wh... who... whosoever... unmasks... the Dragon of the Deep...,' he stammered.

Ah, so thunderstruck perhaps. But not yet wonderstruck, awestruck... Well she could change that in a jiffy.

'Wait,' she murmured. With a single graceful movement she slipped her swimsuit straps off her golden brown shoulders and free of her arms, her breasts lunging free. And then bent down and stepped out of it altogether. She straightened up and pushed her hair behind her ears, as he stared at her in disbelief his mouth working soundlessly.

Oh God! Right in front of him! A completely naked whole girl! No, woman! No, lady! No, *Maya!* Naked from head to toe! Back and front! Her brown body gleaming wet, water running down her thighs and hips, dark wet tendrils of hair curling around those round, round brown breasts, heaving gently. And that dark mysterious bespangled patch where her thighs met, with its curls sparkling with drops of water like diamonds. She rolled up her swimsuit into a ball and tossed it on the beach. For a long moment they stared at each other perhaps a yard apart.

He gulped.

'Who... who... whoso.... whosoever unmasks the Dr... Dragon of the Deep...,' he squeaked again valiant till the end...

'...shall engulf him in her arms forever, you silly goose!' she finished huskily, stepping forwards and wrapping her arms around him, squeezing him against her as tightly as she could.

He couldn't believe how incredibly soft and smooth her body was – surely it was the softest thing in the world! But what the hell had happened? And right in the middle of a naval battle! Hell he gave a damn, he was with Maya, his most wonderful, beautiful person in the world, that's all that mattered. He tightened his arms around her. She seemed to be melting into him...

'Come on, she whispered, "let's get ashore!" She laid him down gently on the exercise mat and lay astride him, propping herself up by an elbow, her breasts gently nuzzling his chest and face (they were deliciously salty), and gazed down at him. 'Now I've got you where I want you,' she said smiling.

'Yash! Yash! Are you okay? Hey you Dragon of the Deep, are you okay? Do you copy?'

The Dragon of the Deep had passed out!

A wavelet licked her ankle and she scooped up a palmful of water and sprinkled it on his face. Within moments, his eyes flickered open.

'You, you...,' he stammered weakly, smiling dazedly up at her. 'What happened? I think you... I think you just *nuked* me! It was... it was like we... was...!'

She kissed his face all over. 'Yes,' she said softly, kissing him helplessly, relentlessly almost, 'yes!'

Another wavelet came in and washed over them.

'I think the tide is coming in,' she said, 'we'd better get up on the ledge.' She took his hand and helped him up, scooping up her swimsuit and robe in one hand. The ships of the great navy had all run aground, and still naked, they collected them and put them in the sack. Together they dragged the exercise mat back up on the ledge and lay down side by side, staring at each other. Then she turned onto her back and looked up at the hot blue sky, its searing heat belied by its rich all-encompassing blueness. For nearly half an hour they lay quietly, and then he reached out his hand tentatively towards her breast half-expecting it to be slapped away, and still not quite believing what had just happened. But it had, because she took it, kissed it and firmly placed it on her breast cupping his fingers over it. He rolled over and stared at her. His eyes widened in horror.

'You're bleeding!' he exclaimed and she propped herself up and looked down at her thighs quickly.

'Not there, here!' he said, touching her breast gently. 'I think I bit you!' He leant forwards and licked the neat coronet of ruby droplets. 'I'm sorry!'

'Umm... it doesn't matter!'

'Maya?' he asked tentatively, 'what happened? I mean down there on the beach? How did… how did you…'

She shrugged. 'I don't know, Yash, it just happened I guess. Maybe I just wanted to meet the dragons on your bum. Maybe… I just wanted to hug you for being… um for just being *you!* I can't really explain it!'

'I am me,' he said simply, 'I'm nobody else! And I'm glad it happened that way. Otherwise, I would have had to happen it and I was so scared…'

'You would have had to "happen it?" What do you mean? Happen what?' But of course she knew what he meant.

'Um… I wanted to happen what happened very badly,' he explained and then smiled happily. 'And then you made it happen. Just like that! You're really great!'

'And you're really a nut case! You could have… er… hugged me anytime you know.'

She was languid now, melting slowly, blissful. He was gazing at her again, his eyes running over her body frankly curious.

'No girl has ever seen me naked before,' he admitted. 'Everywhere, I mean!' he clarified. And added hastily, 'And I haven't seen any girl naked either. Live, I mean. Both up and down. And don't want to. Excepting you!'

'Thanks.'

'Yash, do you think I'm gaunt?' she asked unexpectedly.

'What?' he said, raising his eyebrows, 'No, but you do look like a basset hound sometimes.'

'Thanks. So then I'm lugubrious?'

'Lugu-lugu-what?'

'Okay! Never mind! And broody? Do I look broody?'

He stared at her walleyed for a moment, and then tucked his elbows into his ribs and nodded seriously.

'Wakwakwak!' he clucked suddenly, getting up and doing a chicken run up and down the ledge. 'Wakwakwak! Broody chick, broody chick, broody chick! Wakwakwak wakwakwak!'

'Idiot!' She giggled sitting up and placing her arms around her knees, 'now stop jumping about and sit down here beside me. You're making me nervous. I don't want you falling off the ledge or something.'

She rolled over and lay on her tummy and he gazed at her bottom, enthralled.

'Come on, oh Dragon of the Deep,' she said, rolling over again and opening up her arms to him. 'Stop staring at my butt and come on.' She opened her arms to him.

'Kiss me oh Dragon of the Deep,' she whispered, 'kiss me!'

He puckered his lips ferociously, shut his eyes and kissed – and missed. (Not the right time to show and tell he hadn't kissed a chickie in his life!) And never saw the smile on her face as she drew him to her and began kissing him again.

Below them in the cove the sea chuckled and gurgled knowingly – their sweet time would all too soon be over.

Maya awoke first, about an hour later and sat up. She smiled as she leant over him again to look at the time, remembering the last time she had done so. Again, they still had some time before it was time to get back.

'Wake up, sleepyhead! Let's eat!' she said, shaking him gently. 'I'm famished!'

Tousled he sat up. She took out the fruit and tins she had brought and they ate ravenously. Then they sat out on the edge of the ledge, their legs dangling down, and stared out at the sea, the sun warm on their bare bodies. As they had done for millennia, the breakers roared shorewards, rearing up to display their power before curling over glassily and crashing with that deep booming thump. On the rocks surrounding the cove, the big green crabs clattered ponderously, and would continue to do so tomorrow, day after and probably forever. The world just went on, without pause as if nothing had changed, nothing wonderful had happened. Oh well! Maya picked up her swimsuit lying crumpled in the sand nearby.

'I'm just going down to have a dip and wash the sand off this,' she said. 'It'll be horribly uncomfortable to wear otherwise! Coming?'

'Sure! And don't be shy!' he called after her, getting up and following. 'You don't have to put it on just yet!'

'Idiot!'

He glanced around. 'Hey Maya, by the way, where are my trunks?' he asked.

'Your trunks?' She looked around blankly, horror slowly dawning as she remembered. She had slipped them off him and in that overheated moment just dropped them into the water. 'Oh my God…,' she said, but unable to stifle a giggle.

'What?'

'They… they must have floated out with the tide!'

'What? You mean I have to go back like this?' He looked down at himself. 'But I can't go back like this!'

'You can wrap your towel around you, no one will know – except me! And I won't tell, maybe!'

'I didn't bring a towel. Did you?'

'No, I have my toweling robe…Maybe you can wear that!'

'Never! Oh, shit, my parents will freak!'

'Don't be shy,' she said coyly, still dissolving into giggles. 'No one will look twice at a naked boy on the beach!'

'My parents will… will exterminate me!' he said, shaking his head dolefully.

'Come here, oh mighty Dragon of the Deep!' She sat down and pulled him down in her lap. 'We'll think of something!'

'Oh God!' he said in a hollow voice, 'you know and I'll probably never see you again after today!' And added sepulchrally, 'and maybe I'll become a father!'

'Nonsense! Father, my foot!' Maya frowned. But if… but if… She had taken no precautions, nor had he, because neither had the faintest idea about the miraculous surprise fate had lined up for them that morning. And to go around looking for protection now – that would stir up a hornet's nest. Perhaps she could – very tactfully – ask Sherry. She was quite a girl about town.

'You are coming to this beastly party tonight aren't you?' she asked.

'Oops, I forgot to tell you… my parents won't let me! They want to leave very early for Goa tomorrow morning.'

'Oh, shit. Heck, I'm going to miss you terribly! You're the only person I can be with and talk to in this place, without feeling like a deadbeat!'

'Me too! Maybe we could elope!' He shook his head. 'Or maybe I'll just run away from Goa and come back here and hide. And you can meet me here clandestinely!'

She smiled. 'You know it won't work, you nut,' she said sadly pushing his head away. 'Come on,' she said pushing his head, 'I guess we'd better get back!'

'You forget I'm naked!' he complained. 'I'll only agree to go like this, if you agree to the same condition!'

'Tell you what. I'll run back and fetch you some shorts. I'll tell your parents that you're hiding behind the rocks because you tore your trunks on their sharp edges or something!'

He brightened up. 'Great idea!' he said.

She stood up to put on her swimsuit. And paused, staring at one end of the cove.

'Yash – look there at the corner of the cove…! Near those rocks!'

He followed her gaze and a bright smile lit up his face. 'My swimming trunks!' he exclaimed delightedly, 'the tide must have brought them back!'

'For your kind information, the Queen of the Sirens ordered the sea to return them to you!' she said. 'Now you owe her big time again!' He ran and fetched them.

'You know, Maya I'm going to miss you,' he said, burying his face in her breasts again. 'Like I told you, every time I meet anyone nice, we leave town! And tomorrow we are going to stupid Goa! Why does it always have to be like that?'

'And I'm going to miss you and your nonsense too! Try to come back here. I'm here for another month…'

'I will!'

They put on their costumes, and trudged back in silence to the resort.

Hari Shanbagh, with his 50X digital camcorder had missed out on an opportunity of a lifetime.

7

Back at the cottage the devils began stirring in Maya's head almost immediately after she got back. Thankfully, her mother was not in. Mrs Sabherwal had managed to corral three other bored ladies who had no interest in the beach and played bridge with them and gossiped all day – so there was no interrogation for Maya to face. Except for the one that was being ruthlessly conducted by her own team of poison dart interrogators sent straight from the devil.

Exactly what madness had gone down that morning at Razor Rock 3?

What on earth had made her slip Yash's swimming trunks off like that? But she was already smiling haplessly at the memory. *Anyone* would have done that – it had been beyond temptation. It was Yash!

But afterwards? She had stepped out of her own swimsuit without the slightest shred of embarrassment (which she had not felt even during yesterday's 'wardrobe malfunction' which, she now admitted with a wry smile indeed must have been a Freudian slip!), as if it had been the most natural thing to do – because, because, she gulped as the truth came out, she had *wanted* to. Just as she had wanted to take him into her arms and kiss and hold him close and tight. She had wanted to… all along… since when?

She shook her head. She was crazy! She was seventeen, he was just about (a rather small) fifteen – she wasn't even sure how old exactly. Okay so it was just two years really, which was no big deal, but it seemed so much more. He came up to her shoulders and had such a baby face! She really was a siren – a seductress from the sea who lured and consumed young boys for breakfast! Or had he been to blame? Had he worked his wily wicked charms on her and drawn her irresistibly to him? But then she remembered 'awestruck, wonderstruck and thunderstruck,' and stared at her face in the mirror and shook her head. 'I started it,' she admitted. 'I started it!' And now, and now she could even be pregnant! She shook her head exasperatedly, for Christ's sake he was just fifteen – not old enough to make anyone pregnant surely! That horrible thought belonged to the trashcan. Recycle bin, another little devil whispered, burying its poison dart accurately and maliciously. Recycle bin.

But why? Why had she started it? Because… because he was Yash came the helpless answer. What choice had she in the matter? Well then, he was to blame after all for being Yash! But her poison dart devils would not let her leave it at that.

'What's the matter with me?' she asked herself fiercely. 'What's wrong with me? I should be swooning over muscle-bound hunks like Donny, not chasing small (but he was sturdy and quite strong – he had lugged his trolley and bag all that way) boys and their frisky tadpoles! I'm hopeless!' Or was it… was it because hunks like Donny and his friends found her 'gaunt' and 'broody' and didn't have 'accounts' (whatever they meant by that) for fairness creams? No! Never! She would rather be running naked after Yash any time than hang out with Donny-type hunks.

'And now I'll probably never see him again,' she sniffed dolefully, wiping her eyes. But somehow she could not bring herself to believe that entirely, which was good because it would have upset her even more if she had.

'I'm going to put away what happened in a memory safe,' she said becoming somewhat maudlin, 'and wait for him to open it again one day!'

Another little devil spoke up maliciously: but did he, did he feel the same way? God knows she hadn't given him a chance in hell

– she had just been all over him, smothering him, devouring him! But of course he did – she shut her eyes remembering the shining delight in his eyes when she had showed up at the rock that morning. And later he had admitted that he had wanted to do to her what she had done to him but had been too scared. 'He does like me!' she convinced herself. Very, very much she hoped.

And now, now there was this ghastly party to think about. She flung open her cupboard and gazed at the heaps of shorts and T-shirts hanging there with increasing dismay. Pack for a month, her mother had said, and so she had – but she had packed for a month *on the beach!* And apart from that slinky red miniskirt number, and two dressy sleeveless tops – one black (which she had already worn, so could not possibly wear again so soon) and the other cream (with a risky neckline) – there was nothing she could conceivably wear to a party! 'Damn!' she exclaimed, wondering if she should borrow something from Sherry. Never! One, they were different sizes and two Sherry would really think she hailed from the boondocks. Red miniskirt and sleeveless pale cream top (albeit with a risky neckline) it would have to be.

She was ready at eight and rang Sherry at the villa to ask whether she should come down as yet.

'Maya darling but it's only eight!' Sherry squealed down the line, sounding sleepy. 'I'll give you a call when we're ready to leave – or maybe send Hari down to fetch you!'

'Come here, Maya let me brush your hair!' her mother called, glad to see her ready and spruced up. 'I hope you shampooed it properly. All that seawater will ruin it!'

It was just past ten and she had dozed off in her chair when Hari – dressed in black – showed up on a motorcycle.

'We're going on that?' Maya asked, her heart sinking.

He grinned. 'My chariot awaits!' he said. 'We go back to the villa first – the others are waiting there.' Reluctantly she climbed on behind him.

'How was your day?' he bellowed, turning around, putting his face far too close to hers. God! He's been eating breath fresheners wholesale all day, she thought, recoiling from the sharp peppermint tang.

'It was fine, thanks!'

'And the mid... little boyfriend?'

'Um... you mean Yash? He can't come – he's off to Goa tomorrow and his parents want to leave very early. And he's not my boyfriend.' Much, much more than just that and wouldn't you like to know about it pus-face, but of course she never said that.

'Okay, no need to take offense! But you should meet some great people tonight. A whole bunch of them have biked down from Bombay!'

There were about a dozen motorbikes parked rakishly about in the parking lot, with people swarming aimlessly in the garden, talking and laughing. A small bus belonging to the resort stood parked outside, with Srinivas (the driver who had brought them down from Mumbai) standing next to it.

Sherry, in mauve jeans and matching tank top, which stopped way above where it ought to have, tripped up and put her arms around her shoulders.

'Maya! You're looking wicked! I wish I tanned like that! Hey guys! Everyone! Gather around!' she squealed loudly, clapping her hands. 'I want you to meet my cousin Maya from Delhi!'

'Hi Maya!' The chorus of voices was casual but friendly, and Maya's spirits rose. Maybe they were nice kids after all. Maybe she was being uncharitable.

'Right darling, I'll do a quick round of introductions here before we leave – it'll be impossible at Billy's place what with his music and all!' Sherry took Maya by the arm and led her through the milling crowd.

'This is Ajay and Shyamola – they're both models, Vijay – hey VJ what are you into now? Sweety – she's a crack interior decorator, that's Neha – she's with that fab new rag, *Hot 'n' Nasty*.' She giggled,

'I think Hari has the hots for her,' she said and went on, 'Ankit and Shenzy – both aspiring to be DJs, Donny – you met him at the shoot remember, Reema…' But Maya had lost track long before. Arunda was there too with his ponytail. And regretfully, and too late, Maya realized that she could have quite easily worn one of her faded denim shorts and T-shirts – everyone here was dressed for the beach it seemed, excepting her! Idiot! She should have asked Sherry at least, what was appropriate!

The guys were gunning their motorbikes; most had their girlfriends along. Hari came up to Maya grinning.

'You'll ride with me!' he grinned, handing her a helmet.

'But… but what about Sherry?'

'She'll catch a ride with someone don't worry! Donny probably! She's his mermaid!'

'Oh!' He leaned towards her and squeezed her arm and winked.

'And you can be mine!' As if he were bestowing a favour on her.

At that moment, Pankaj Mama stepped out into the veranda and clapped his hands for attention. 'Hi everybody! Helmets on everyone!' he shouted and there was a roar of applause and a sea of helmets waved at him.

'Right Uncle!'

'And remember, no boozing and riding!'

'Right, Uncle!'

Sherry came by clinging to Donny's arm. She glanced at her father up on the top of the steps and made a face. 'It's so embarrassing! He does this every time! Really! She turned to Maya. 'You okay Maya?' she asked. 'Don't ride too fast Hari, you know how bumpy the road is!'

'I know, I know, you don't have to lecture me.'

'What's with the mini-bus?' Maya asked. Srinivas had got into the bus and started it up. Sherry made another exasperated face and then giggled.

'That's what we call the paddy wagon! Daddy insists we take it along. So if anyone er… has too much beer and goes to sleep they can be brought back safely!' She snorted. 'Can you imagine, in this day and age, being chaperoned by a bus!' She winked, 'but poor Daddy doesn't know the half of what goes on in the back of that bus sometimes!'

'Come on, Maya, let's go!'

Hari helped her (unnecessarily) to strap on her helmet – too tight she soon discovered – and she got on. He kicked the bike to life and set off with a jerk. Maya clutched on to the sides for dear life. 'Hang on to my waist,' he shouted, but that was one thing she would not do.

At least not yet. They rode down the dark deserted coastal road, two-by-two at a comfortable pace, the bikes throbbing and burbling happily along, their headlights lighting up the narrow road ahead. Someone began a song and soon a ragged chorus, interspersed by roars of laughter rent the air. The party had already begun. Behind them, Srinivas followed in the paddy wagon. Suddenly, Hari veered off onto the bumpy verge, and waved the others on ahead. Srinivas slowed as he came abreast, but Hari waved him on.

'Theek hai!' he shouted. 'I've just got something in my eye!' He had taken off his helmet and was blinking owlishly. 'I'll catch up!' The bus lumbered on ahead. Maya looked into the surrounding darkness, her heart beginning to beat nervously fast. It seemed too close around them, isolating them in the pool of light thrown by the bike. Still she could re-adjust the damn helmet at least. She took it off and shook her hair free. Hari had pulled a pencil torch out of a pocket and handed it to her, still blinking.

'Have a look Maya! I think some damn insect got in through my visor!'

He brought his face close up to hers. She shone the beam into his piggy pale brown eye, and noticed it was neither red nor watering. Just blinking owlishly – and obscenely it seemed – at her.

'There seems to be nothing in it,' she said.

'Come closer. Blow gently on it,' he said. But he deliberately would not keep still. 'You'll have to hold my head,' he said as if exasperated with himself for being fidgety. So she clutched a fistful of hair none too gently and debated whether she should blow a tempest into that leering eye. In the end, she just blew gently and with growing horror realized that he had slipped an arm around her waist and was trying to press himself against her, his mouth hovering dangerously close to hers. She pushed him away and backed off. Then her eye fell on a bottle of water on the bike's carrier bag.

'Wait a sec,' she said, retrieving it and unscrewing it and waving it in his face. A stream of water leapt out, straight into his face, making him stagger back. 'Oops! I'm sorry! But here, you can wash your eye out with this!'

'It's fine,' he said, wiping his face with a handkerchief and leaping back on the bike. 'Come on, get on we'd better catch up with the others or they'll come looking.' She got on, and before she could put on her helmet, the bike had leapt forward.

'Hang on!' he shouted. 'And enjoy the wind in your hair!'

He was riding at such speed over such a bad road, she had no choice but to lean forward and hang on to him – or else risk falling off.

Twenty minutes later, they roared into Billy's house. Maya had just closed her eyes for most part of the journey, trying to ignore the feeling of Hari pressing his back against her every few minutes. Her hair was an absolute mess, when she got off, shaken and disheveled and near tears. Sherry spotted her and came up.

'Tsk, tsk, Maya darling you've been riding bareheaded! Papa will be very angry if he knew, but I know, there's nothing quite like it! Come on, now, say hi to Billy!' Sherry had to squeal at the top of her voice, because the music drowned everything. Even the sea.

Billy was a jovial, rotund sardar, with a friendly grin and welcoming manner in knee-length shorts and a batik shirt and a turquoise turban.

'Welcome, my dear!' he bellowed, 'what will you have to drink?' On the lawn, beautifully lit up with lights in the hedges and bushes, the bar had been arranged, around which people were buzzing as thickly as bees around a hive. At the beach end, a powerful sound system had been set up and was throbbing away, with strobe lights already pulsating. A few kids were dancing.

'Come along to the bar, Maya!' Billy bellowed. 'What will you have?'

'Something soft, please,' Maya said, running the comb that Sherry had given her, through her hair. (She had idiotically forgotten to put her compact into her bag.) 'A Coke would be fine!' She looked around. There must have been fifty people at least, tossing back their drinks (some poisonously coloured) and scarfing down the sizzling fried prawns and other snacks piled on the tables. Billy handed her a tall glass of Coke, crowned with crushed ice and grinned. 'Have a good time!' he shouted. 'You'll have to introduce yourself I'm afraid. I don't know half the people here myself!'

The party had been arranged out in the garden of Billy's house, which was virtually on the beach. Maya wandered around a bit, at a loss, smiling vacuously at the kids who bumped into her. Most just greeted her with a breathless 'hi' and went on their way – usually to the bar. Sherry had disappeared somewhere – and Hari was huddled around three or four guys, sniggering and laughing. Once, they looked in her direction and she dodged nimbly behind a couple busily engrossed in 'snogging' as Yash would have put it. At last she wandered down to the gate and gazed out at the breakers, silvery in the faint moonlight, as they raced in, broke and tumbled. Here, the music was just a little less intrusive and she wondered if she should step out into the cool sand.

'Hey, Maya, what are you doing out there all on your own?' She turned. It was Hari again, knocking back something purple, blinking thickly. 'Come here, there's someone I want you to meet!' There were two unshaven looking guys with him, both in cut-off vests and jeans – one of them wearing very snazzy scarlet sneakers indeed. Both were prickly bald. Hanging on to them were two skimpily-clad girls in skirts and tank tops, giggling at one another and running their hands through their hair.

'Guys, Neha and Zabby, meet my cousin Maya from Delhi' Hari grinned. 'Maya, these two thugs are Rohit and Sohail. Maya's all by herself and mooning because her little boyfriend couldn't make it! So you better make it up to her!'

'Oh is that so? You poor thing!'

'What does he do?' asked the girl called Neha.

'Class IV in school!' Hari hooted, slapping his thighs with mirth.

'He's just kidding…' Maya stammered, but she knew her face was going red. (But there were advantages to being dusky at night!) 'It's nothing like that!'

'Maya's also still in school,' Hari went on garrulously (and why did Maya get the feeling that he had just added, 'and will be there forever' even though he hadn't said it?). 'She's special so look after her well, you guys. And she's a crack runner!' He turned to one of the scruffy fellows and grinned. 'I'll bet she can outrun you Rohit! You see, Rohit here is another crackpot jogger type,' he explained to Maya, snaking an arm around her.

'Yeah, yeah,' Rohit nodded good-naturedly. 'Sure, sure!'

'Seriously man, you should just see her go on the beach. Like a gazelle!'

'Hari, stop it…'

'Now you're embarrassing her!' the girl called Neha said, taking her hand and smiling frighteningly through her blood-scarlet lipstick.

'But she does,' said Hari in his most earnest, do-gooder-voice. 'She takes part in all these charity marathon runs…'

Rohit eyes crinkled with interest. 'Oh,' he said. 'So what's your best time?'

'Best time? Oh… I don't know really!' Maya mumbled. 'I never check'

'Never check? Oh, I see.' The interest was already flickering out of Rohit's eyes.

'Say, you know what?' Hari put a protective arm around Maya and drew her close again. 'Maya here will challenge you to a run on the beach tonight. We'll pace out what – one kilometre or something on the beach and she'll race you! What do you say, Maya? Show him! Show him what Delhi chicks are made of!'

'No, no… Hari, please!' But deep inside her something flickered. If she could show this silly prattling crowd of wannabe DJs and fashion designers how she could run, maybe they'd not be so condescending (frankly, this was more imagined than real as she hadn't as yet interacted with anyone at the party) to her – treating her like a pigtailed schoolgirl (even if that's what she still was). Even if she couldn't beat this Rohit guy, giving him a good run for his money would be enough to shut them up and open their eyes.

'So what do you say, Maya?' Hari went on. 'Are you on? Come on, be a sport!'

'Umm…' It was a nice night for a run anyway. And maybe she could run all the way back to Shanbagh resort from here and into Yash's arms! Idiot! 'Umm…'

'She's on!' Hari whooped. 'Great!' It gave him another excuse to hug her and plant a couple of kisses on her cheeks.

'Come on, you guys,' Neha yelled. 'You can run your races later. Let's dance!'

'As you have challenged me,' Rohit said smiling, 'will you dance with me first?' But there was a glint in his eye, which Maya didn't quite like.

Twenty minutes later (and dancing, Maya discovered was a nice way of limbering up for a run) the music suddenly stopped. The crowed buzzed puzzled and then Hari was on the mike.

'Listen up, everyone! We have special entertainment on tonight! Instead of the usual boozing and smoking and getting stoned and disappearing behind the rocks, which all of you like to do, we have something wholesome lined up for a change. My cousin Maya, who's down from Delhi and is a crack long-distance runner, has just challenged our very own Rohit for a run on the beach. Over a distance of one kilometre – five hundred metres up and five hundred metres down!'

Cheers and whistles greeted the announcement – as well as a few catcalls and hoots.

'Maya, come on up here darling – let them see you!'

She made her way up to the mike and stood next to Hari, almost dead of embarrassment. Then Rohit jogged up beside her casually and waved to the crowd. They roared and hooted back.

'So Maya would you like a handicap?' Hari asked, smiling at her as if he were the keeper of the gates of heaven.

Maya shook her head. 'No,' she said, 'no handicap, please!'

There were cheers and screams from the girls, and more hoots from the guys.

'So would you like to give Rohit a handicap then?' Hari asked, as the crowd cheered and whistled and stamped their feet, really getting into the spirit of the competition.

'No,' she said. 'That won't be fair either!'

More cheers and screams from the girls, and boos from the guys, but it didn't matter really. 'I would like to see the course though!' she added. 'Where we're going to run.'

They poured out onto the beach, with flashlights and lanterns, Billy leading the way. 'I know just the course,' he said, 'I jog it every morning!'

It seemed to be pretty straightforward. 'You see those clumps of rocks,' Billy said pointing along the beach. Maya realized it was the same beach where Sherry's ad film had been shot. There were three widely separated heaps of rocks, arranged more or less in a straight line down the beach, parallel to the shoreline. 'You start from here, run past the middle clump, then circle around the third clump and return. It's about five hundred metres, so back and forth will be one kilometre.' Even better, was that at the 'finish', there were two more or less parallel sets of rocks (like grandstands of the Flintstone era) on either side, between which the runners would pass, and on which already the partygoers were clambering and screaming when they encountered crabs or slipped on the moss. Just beyond the finish line, a huge tidal pool glimmered in the moonlight, and here more rocks were nicely arranged in steps, on which the crowd now settled, glasses and cans in hand. It would be like running into a cul-de-sac at the finish, Maya thought, with your audience cheering from three sides. But the glimmering rock pool meant you had to pull up very sharply after crossing the finish or risk getting your feet and clothes wet.

The moon was up, bathing the beach in a pale silvery light, but Billy was a stickler for detail and very particular about safety. He organized a set of emergency lanterns to be set up on bamboo poles at intervals along the course, so that the 'track' was lit up as brightly as possible. Privately Maya thought it would have been better to just run in the faint moonlight. And suddenly realized that she had no running shorts. Shoes didn't matter because she ran barefoot.

'Sherry,' she said. 'I don't have anything to run in!'

Billy, who had overheard, grinned. 'Well I could lend you my shorts, except about four of you will fit in them!'

There was nothing for it. She would have to run in her skirt and top or not at all. And there was no way she could back out now.

Hari and Rohit and some of his other friends were in a huddle near the 'grandstands', and looking as if they were measuring distances out with lengths of rope. Every now and then one or the other would break into guffaws of laughter, and start shoving and pushing before being cuffed and hushed by the others. They'd already had more than enough to drink, Maya thought primly. Making fools of themselves like that.

'Okay,' Billy said glancing up at the moon. 'I think it'll be it's brightest in about half an hour – so shall we have the start then?'

'Right on!'

'Come on, let's go back to the bar!'

He herded his guests back into the garden. Maya sat down quietly wondering if she had done the right thing. She could see some of this extremely hip crowd looking at her curiously. Hari came over and patted her thigh.

'Don't worry,' he said. 'Nothing to be nervous about! Here,' he said handing her a bright orange coloured drink. 'A mocktail of fruit juices – to ginger you up for the run!' He lowered his voice and glanced around. 'It's also an energy drink – it'll pep you up for the race.' And grinned, 'We don't have dope testing facilities here, so you're safe!'

She accepted the drink and had to admit it tasted wonderful.

'Thanks,' she said. 'It's really good! Fruity!'

About forty minutes later they trooped back out onto the beach. Rohit jogged on the spot and waved his arms about like a champion boxer entering the ring. Maya kicked off her sandals and wriggled her toes in the cool sand. Whatever else, she would enjoy running – she was feeling really good. And confident like she had never felt before.

'Hey, we better get a move on, the tide's coming in!' someone yelled.

'Don't worry. It just about reaches here at its maximum,' Billy said. He called out to the runners. 'Okay, you guys, note you have to dodge past these big pools and stop before the one at the end or you'll splash the audience, so don't run with your eyes closed, please! Right, are we ready?'

'Yeah!' came the roar from the crowd. Of course, about twenty-five more people had now decided to join in, so it was beginning to look like a genuine mini-marathon.

'On your marks, get setttt... Go!' yelled Billy in a stentorian voice, as Sherry clutched him.

'I hope she beats him,' she said knocking back the contents of her glass. 'I hope she beats him! It'll really make her day!'

And Maya was off. Several runners surged ahead of her amidst screams from the onlookers, but tailed off by the middle clump of rocks, reeling and clutching their sides, whooping and gasping and laughing. (Arunda and Donny were one of the early drop-offs she noted with satisfaction.) But right at her side, Rohit pounded along, steadily, easily, his scarlet runners flashing like splashes of blood. Suddenly, unaccountably, Maya weaved and staggered and then corrected her direction and regained her balance. What the hell was that about? She blinked and shook her head from side to side, trying to clear it. Just what was the matter with her? Why was she woozy and feeling fuzzy?

'You okay?' Rohit grunted, watching her and still cantering along easily.

'Yes, thanks!' she said. A gust of cool breeze from the sea cleared her head like a fog being blown away.

That energy drink she had had! Obviously it hadn't suited her! Idiot that she was for accepting it! (It had been spiked with a hefty shot of vodka actually.)

They were still neck and neck at the halfway point, and Maya had just begun to enjoy herself again. She glanced down the beach, trying to decide when she should make her move. She could hear Rohit grunting now as he kept pace.

Okay, she thought, just beyond the middle clump – that's when I'll take off – about a hundred-and-fifty metres before the finish line. At the speed she was running she knew she'd have the reserves to put on a good burst. But before she knew it, Rohit had already surged past her and a roar erupted from the crowd. But Maya had heard his whooping gasps as he went past, and smiled. Mr Rohit was fast running out of steam (and had probably drunk too many multicoloured drinks). She made her move just where she had planned to and was already gaining on him by then. She passed him swiftly as the roars from the crowd drowned even the thumping and hissing of the sea.

'Maayaa! Maayaa! Maayaa!'

She was in her element now, running fast and cleanly and easily, not even minding her skirt swishing up and down. About fifty metres from the finish, she heard thudding footsteps behind her, and a roar from the crowd. She glanced over her shoulder. Rohit was catching up fast! Maybe she had relaxed unconsciously, thinking that the race was over, a little too early. She put on a burst of speed as she entered the 'grandstand' section and weaved between a few small pools. Several of the partygoers had brought their cameras – including of course Hari who was crouched on the rocks beyond the finish line, a new strobe blazing away. Just twenty-five metres to go now, and she could hear Rohit hard on her heels, breathing hard. A wavelet curled around and refilled the pool at the far end beyond the finish line. She had to admit, he was stretching her to the limit. Like all good runners, she put on a final desperate burst of speed and lunged forward.

And found herself suddenly airborne as she tripped over the nearly invisible jute rope drawn taut across the track. She took off and landed, face down, with a tremendous splash in the pool the wavelet had just brimmed, her arms outspread – rather like Yash had that morning, so many aeons ago. There came a loud ripping sound and her slinky red skirt flew up behind her folding completely over her back as she crash-landed like a plane doing a bellyflop. There was a sudden hush from the crowd, then as she rose, trembling, and was splashed head to toe again as Rohit charged past. A roar again, and then clearly the first of the giggles (and rather drunken) snickers and sniggers, from the onlookers as they stared at her. The cameras continued to flash and Hari's strobe was unrelenting, blinding her as it had blinded Yash.

She was dripping from head to toe, her top completely ripped open down the front, her breasts heaving behind her bra, now totally transparent.

'Maya!' screamed Sherry leaping down from the rocks. 'Are you all right darling?'

But Hari was already at her side, gallantly putting his camera aside and trying to button the front of her ripped top again, and pretending as if he didn't know where his hands were going. He took out his handkerchief and began rubbing her down, as someone in the crowd began wolf-whistling raucously.

'I'm… I'm…,' she tried desperately to hold back the sobs that were rising and wishing she could die.

They crowded around her and now Hari, ever solicitous smoothened her skirt down, running his hand along her bottom as he did. Then someone brought a towel from the house, and Sherry wrapped her up in it. Her bedraggled skirt clung to her hips, and she heard the snide, 'nice ass!' as she stumbled away helped by Sherry and Neha. They escorted her back to the house as the party began to get going again.

Her top was ruined. There was no way she could wear it again. So they borrowed a T-shirt from Billy – and she was grateful for its voluminous bulk. She waited and dried her hair as Sherry wrung and then ironed her bra and skirt as dry as possible. And she never noticed the strange way that Neha had begun looking at her…

'I don't want to go back out,' she begged. She'd been humiliated by this lot, virtually stripped naked by them. Ogled at and photographed. She might be on the net by tomorrow for the world to see…

She recalled Hari and Rohit and their friends fiddling with the rope before the race and realized what had happened. They had set her up! They had done this deliberately – to get their kicks and to humiliate and embarrass her.

She thought of Yash and his simpleton games with his ships and galleons and forts (well those could get pretty exciting too!) and wept.

As the party wound down some hours later, (exhausted, she had fallen asleep in Billy's bedroom) Neha accosted Hari and looked him up and down.

'Your little cousin, she gets around, eh?'

'What?'

'Well, I hope you haven't been fooling around with her…'

'Neha! I'm her brother for God's sake. She sends me *rakhi* every year!'

'Well, if you haven't someone has! Ah, yes you mentioned the little boyfriend who couldn't make it…'

'What are you talking about?'

'Darling she had a neat arc of tooth-marks on her right breast, that's what I'm talking about! Love bites!'

'Love bites? Impossible! How do you know?'

'I can recognize a love bite when I see one, darling. And you can see for yourself the next time you try and dry her with your hankie.' Neha arched an eyebrow and winked.

He looked dazed. So, Maya and that pipsqueak midget... that's what they'd been doing behind that rock! But this, this could have happened only today! If he'd been around… those damn *Instantnews!* people had screwed his chances of getting a scoop of a lifetime good and proper. Oh the irony of it!

'My God! That little half-pint bastard! I'll wring his neck the next time I see him!'

'Hey, don't get so uptight big brother. It takes two to tango – and if I recall you had your paws all over her when she had her little accident! Groping her good!'

'I was just helping her up!' Neha raised another eyebrow drifted away, leaving him indignant and outraged; yes he'd missed his great ticket to fame and fortune!

But from now on, Maya would never be able to put a foot on that beach without his knowing about it. He looked at his camcorder. Well, he'd got some hot close-ups today, that was some consolation. And a real bonus, the way her top had split open. The plan had gone off perfectly. She had entertained them all, even if it had embarrassed poor Billy somewhat. Of course she had insisted on travelling back with Srinivas in the mini-bus, and not on his bike. Sherry (giggling rather excessively by now) kept her company, as did five other guests who had completely passed out.

It was getting on to 3 a.m. when Maya crawled into bed and drew up the sheets. The black limerick presented itself, readymade as always, almost at once:

Like a fool I thought I could win
When I heard cheers and the din
But they wanted to strip me
To ogle and flip me
So they tripped me up by the shin!

8

Maya awoke at nearly eight-thirty the next morning to find her mother bustling around putting clothes into a suitcase. She sat up in bed – and the events of the previous night came flooding back like someone pouring a sack of wet cement into her stomach. And Yash, he'd have been long gone … and she had missed saying goodbye to him. Did yesterday morning really happen? Even a million years ago?

'So how was the party, dear?' her mother asked. 'You came back very late! I would have been very worried but I knew you were with Hari and Sherry. Did you enjoy yourself?'

'Why are you packing, Ma?' she asked. 'Are we going back to Delhi?' Maybe that would be the best thing now.

'Papa has had to bring forward his trip to London,' her mother said. 'I'm leaving for Bombay this afternoon to join him; we catch the flight tonight. You'll stay here – with Hari and Sherry!'

'You mean here – or at their house?' she asked, her heart sinking. She couldn't bear to stay with her cousins.

'With them, of course,' her mother said.

'Ma, please can I stay here at the cottage?' she begged. 'I'll go over for meals and stuff but would like to sleep and bathe here. We're so well settled.'

'Don't be silly, Maya! How can you possibly sleep here alone at night!' She sniffed and looked at Mathew who was arranging yet another magnificent breakfast. 'Isn't that so Mathew?'

And again as always, it was smiling Mathew who came to her rescue.

'If you like madam, my wife Maria will come and look after Maya miss and sleep here!' he offered. He smiled and winked at Maya. 'And not to worry madam, Maria is very strict about timings!'

'Ma, you know I'll never be able to share a room with Sherry! She comes and goes at all odd hours – and has her modelling friends over from Bombay every other day. And maybe I'll disturb her too! It won't be fair to her – as it is she's spending so much time with me.'

Mrs Sabherwal glanced at her pensively and surprisingly gave in without a fight. Actually her mind was more on her darling genius Jayant. She couldn't believe she would be fussing all over him tomorrow at this time. Also she hadn't at all liked how late Maya had got back last night and had indeed been quite anxious. Hari and Sherry were responsible children she was sure, and would look after Maya, but 3 a.m. was 3 a.m. and no child ought to be awake at that hour. Also, Sherry was a bit scatterbrained even if she was very sweet but she certainly didn't want Maya to be coming and going 'at all hours'. For once, there appeared to be some sense in what Maya had suggested.

'Oh, okay!' she said exasperatedly, 'I'll tell Pankaj Mama that you want to be on your own! And Mathew, send Maria over so I can have a word with her please!'

Vet her, you mean Maya thought uncharitably. But thanks Ma, all the same.

'Very well, madam,' Mathew said. He went into the kitchenette and emerged with a brown paper package.

'Miss Maya, this is for you. Mr Yash left this for you at the reception before leaving this morning.'

'Oh!' She took the package her cheeks beginning to burn. 'Th… thanks Mathew.'

She took the package to her room and tore it open.

In a clear plastic box inside, resplendent in a new coat of lacquer and varnish lay *HMS Victory*, her masts folded neatly along her deck. Breathlessly Maya opened the box and unfolded the note that had been placed on the deck.

> Hi Maya, this is for you. I've repaired her the best I can and given her a new coat of paint and varnish. Don't worry, I love doing things like this, so it wasn't any bother, but I took special care to make this job special for you. She's ready for her next battle. I wish I wasn't going to Goa but my parents are like gypsies, I tell you. Can't stay in one place. But I'm going to make them come back here somehow – I promise because I really want to er … hug you again like you hugged me (all naked!). Yash.

She took the ship out of the box, and raised the masts. The sails unfurled beautifully. She squinted at the spot where his cannonballs had holed her yesterday and shook her head amazed. Whatever else he might be, gung-ho big talker and wisecrack, Yash was a genuine craftsman – there was no sign that the ship had suffered any damage whatsoever. He must have been up all evening and night fixing her. Carefully she placed the ship on a table and folded up the note as Mathew knocked deferentially at the door.

'Come in,' she said automatically and then pointed out the ship.

'See what he gave me, Mathew,' she said. 'He made it himself.'

'It's a beautiful ship, madam.' Mathew went up to it and examined it. 'If he constructed this himself then he's very good with his hands. Now breakfast is ready!'

She escaped to the beach straight after and to her horror discovered that she had skinned and bruised her shin quite nastily where the rope had tripped her. She had been too upset to notice it last night. Also, her ankle hurt. No running today, though frankly she was too tired and dispirited for even that.

The tide was out, leaving a vast expanse of varnished beach exposed. She wandered about disconsolately, trying to sneak up on the crabs, and picking up the odd gleaming shell, and wondering what she would do all day. Avoid her cousins as much as she could of course for a start, but then what? To her relief she spotted Smita and Asha, playing way out near the tide line. She joined them.

'Hi Smita, hi Asha,' she said smiling at the toddler who as usual was concentrating fiercely on her battles with the waves.

'Hi,' Smita looked up and patted the sand. 'Come sit down! You're looking a little pale this morning. Not feeling well?'

'No, I'm fine,' Maya said, but gulped, glancing at the Rocks. 'Just a little tired from Billy's party!'

'Hmm… hey Asha, don't take your floaters off!'

'She really does love the sea and isn't afraid. I wish I could be like that. Let a wave lift me off my feet and I get major panic attacks!'

'You probably never lived by the sea as a child…'

'You're right.'

'So, Maya what do you do?'

'I'm still in school,' she said colouring. 'I… I was supposed to appear for my boards this year but they didn't send my name up.'

'Oh, I'm sorry about that!'

'I don't know… I'm just not very good at studies I guess,' she said shrugging. Somehow it was easy talking to Smita, you got the feeling that she understood – and didn't try to assess you or judge you all the time. She just accepted what you said.

'Exams are not the only thing in life don't worry! But yes, they do count for rather a lot these days unfortunately!' She smiled, 'So I suppose you have to give them more attention than they deserve! How's your running coming along?'

'I hurt my ankle, so didn't run today,' she said. 'Are the television crew still around?' she asked.

'No, they've gone somewhere for the day, but will be back tomorrow for some meetings with Papa and retakes and something like that!'

'Smita, you don't keep a maid for Asha do you?' Maya asked, 'I've never seen one around and you're always with her yourself.'

Smita shook her head, her eyes turning flinty. 'No,' she said. 'Believe it or not, the last woman I kept actually tried to kidnap Asha. We – I – was very lucky. The police found her within hours. On a train to Bihar!'

'Oh my God, I'm so sorry. You must have been through hell!'

Smita got up briskly and dusted the sand off her hands. 'Okay, let's take this baby seal for a dip, shall we?' she said, and lifted a delighted Asha high up and swooped her through a wave that had just come swishing in. The little girl shouted with laughter.

But soon, Smita and Asha trickled back to their house and Maya found herself tracking slowly towards the Razor Rocks. Maybe Yash had left a ship or galleon there, or hadn't gathered up all of the sailors and pirates that manned them. Perhaps she should check. The little cove was cool and at peace and she sat down in the shallow water, thinking about yesterday and smiling.

From the top of the rock, Hari aimed his camcorder down and extended the zoom. His eyes nearly popped out of his head, as Maya slowly lowered the straps of her swimsuit in order to put on some sunscreen.

She was smiling as she did so, remembering the look on Yash's face when she had leant over him that first morning and her swimsuit had come adrift. For a brief second, her breasts were exposed as she glanced down at her 'love bite' (healing beautifully), but poor Hari's hands were shaking so much by now, that all he got was blurred shots of her foot and a fleeting glimpse of breast.

'Oh my God!' he whispered. 'I just need to bide my time and, and …she'll take everything off! She has to!'

His foot slipped and a rock rolled down. Maya looked up sharply. For a second her heart leapt – had Yash somehow come back? But there was no further sound. She got to her feet and smiled. So maybe the little fellow was ducking behind some rocks, waiting for a chance to give her a surprise. Quietly she began climbing up the rocks, past the ledge where they had been just yesterday. She got to the top and stared in surprise.

Hari was bending low over a rock pool, his camcorder at his eye.

'Oh!' she exclaimed. 'Hari what are you doing here?' She tucked her robe around her instinctively. He turned in mock surprise.

'Maya! Oh, so here you are! Actually I'm making a film on life in rock pools. It's amazing, really, the creatures you can see here. Come here, have a look!'

'No thanks.'

No mention of, no apology for what had happened at the party last night, but just a suggestive snigger or was she imagining things? Well, she hadn't yet apologized for smashing his strobe so maybe that evened things out (and now she had no intention of doing so, forget about replacing it).

As she walked past him, he gave her a look, which made her wonder uneasily if he had indeed been stuck with the *Instantnews!* crew all day, yesterday. If he had been sneaking here yesterday, maybe with the crew (no, they would have made too much noise), with his camera then… then… Her heart sank. The day was turning out to be a complete disaster.

Her mother left that afternoon, and a smiling, bustling Maria took charge of the cottage. She was a plump, curly-haired woman with a brisk manner, and Maya took to her immediately. Sherry took her to the dining room for lunch, but spent most of the time talking to an endless series of friends on her cell-phone. But Sherry at least had the decency to apologize for last night's disaster.

'I'm sorry about your ruined top, darling!' she said. 'Come along with me to the boutique and we'll get you another!'

'No, no, it's all right! Really!'

'Hi!' Hari appeared suddenly and sat down grinning at their table. He winked, 'Heard anything from the mid… little boyfriend as yet?'

'Hari, stop teasing her!' But there was a twinkle in Sherry's eyes too and Maya couldn't understand why.

'I told you, he's not my boyfriend!' Much, much more!

'Rohit was very impressed by your run!'

Well, she had beaten him, hadn't she? Or had she?

'He wanted to see how fast you could accelerate at the end… Pity you fell!'

Hari enjoyed putting the knife in.

She looked at him briefly. 'I didn't fall,' she said coldly, 'I was tripped!'

'Same thing,' he said twisting the knife. 'Same thing!'

How on earth was she going to take another month of this? By the end he'd make her feel like something small and revolting living under a rock. And then, the little genius Jay would arrive and dazzle everyone with his sheer brilliance and posh accent. She might as well shrivel up and die…

She was in this sort of mood early the following morning (despite Maria's attempts to jolly her up), when she went back to the Rocks. She couldn't bear not going there, but when she reached the glinting silvery cove, she was restless. She had waved to Smita and Asha, now down the beach a long way, playing near one of the gleaming bow-shaped sandbanks carved by the waves. Little Asha looked all trussed up in her bright orange floaters. To distract herself, she decided to climb out over the rocks to the mouth of the cove, as far as she could. The tide was still well out, so there was no danger of the cove's little beach being flooded just yet or the rocks being washed over. Cautiously she made her way over the rocks, careful not to slip or cut herself, and enjoying the wind in her hair. She found a comfortable spot and sat down, and gazed out at the sea.

As always, the breakers raced in, smashing themselves to smithereens on the reef, heedlessly, incessantly. 'Really creaming themselves they are!' she thought with a wry chuckle, wishing Yash were beside her with his crooked grin. Yes, creaming themselves good and proper. Like she tended to do to herself with her limericks sometimes. Beyond the reef, the sea glittered and she gasped as a school of flying fish (that's what she thought they were) leapt out of the water like a quiver of silver arrows. How Yash would have loved that!

Again, she thought about that wondrous morning with Yash. Again, the goblins in her mind began heckling. Why didn't she run after someone like Donny, with his biceps and barn-door chest or any of those other hunks with their throbbing motorbikes and snug pillion seats? Why mad small boys like Yash? Because… because guys like Donny didn't look twice at gaunt, broody girls like her while small boys like Yash didn't have a chance, once you engulfed them in your arms like some siren octopus from the deep… True, but also not true: the truth but not the whole truth. Which was what? That Yash was the most comfortable, crazy, wacky person she had ever met and had wanted to be with…

She drew up her knees and rested her chin on them, staring at the waves. They could hypnotize you if you stared at them for too long, she thought with their relentless motion. They charged in roaring, manes flying, then suddenly hushed as they drew themselves up to their full height for their kamikaze assault. And then crashed down with that deep bass boom that could rock your heart from its moorings, and sped in, hissing malevolently, before dying with a sigh at your feet (if you were sensible enough to be at the right distance) in a welter of delicate lace.

Suddenly she stiffened. But what was that… something bright orange, Dayglo orange bobbing swiftly on the waves, borne by the current towards the reef? Just forty or fifty metres in front of her? Something or rather someone rather tiny that surely did not belong there. She stood up and stared and sat down again, as her knees buckled and her blood froze. Asha! Little Asha with her mop of black curls ensconced by her floaters, bobbing rapidly over the waves, on her back, her chubby arms and legs flailing valiantly. Battling the mighty Arabian Sea all by herself. But getting a little frightened now because she hadn't seen her mother's laughing face for a bit, and the waves kept slopping water over her face and into her mouth, making her cough and splutter. In a few seconds, the toddler would be just ten or fifteen metres from her, but heading swiftly for the churning turmoil where the current hit the reef in a welter of foamy confusion. Either the game little toddler would be smashed on the reef, or washed over it by the waves into the wide open expanse of the Arabian Sea to be swallowed at will.

'I am not seeing this I can't be seeing this! I will not see this! If I close my eyes she will just go away.' Maya closed her eyes and opened them again. And spotted the toddler almost immediately again, still buoyant as a vivid orange cork. 'No, this can't be happening! I will not let it happen, shoo Asha, stop teasing me baby! Go away baby go away! Please! Go back to your mom!' A faint high wail drifted on the wind over the roar of the sea. Asha was missing her mom seriously now.

Maya stood up, terrified. She bent down and stretched her arms out towards the baby in a hopeless gesture; Asha might as well have been on the moon for all the good it did. Whimpering, Maya lowered her legs into the sea, clutching at the rock, knowing all the while it was hopeless. She could swim, yes. But… She was waist deep now, still clinging on to the rock, afraid to let go because her toes could not feel the bottom. A wave slapped past roughly, lifting her clean off her feet making her scream and cling on to the rock for dear life. Quickly followed by another which filled her mouth with sea water – they were toying with her like a piece of flotsam or jetsam, jeering and sneering, and buffeting her. Another ruffian nearly tumbled her over, head over heels. And then the biggest one of them all tore her grasp from the rock and she was suddenly tumbling down, down, down, in a welter of silver bubbles amongst the murky depths. This is it, I'm done for, hurry up and get it over and let it not hurt. But spluttering she surfaced – a rock loomed up right in front of her and she grabbed and hugged it. Gibbering with terror she clambered on to it; shaking and trembling, oblivious to the cuts the razor rocks inflicted on her palms and arms. The sea had played with her as if she was a sock in a washing machine. If she had been hurled against the rock, she could have been cut to ribbons. There was no way she was going back in. She watched, white and trembling, her face in her hands, as the baby swept past in front of her, drifting as close as twenty feet away before swirling past. And again, Maya reached out her arms, but they alas were not twenty feet long.

'Oh God, I'm a child murderess now!' she sobbed as the baby swept past and away, 'Oh God that's the last time I'll see Asha and what will I tell Smita?' Blindly she crept back over the rocks like a broken crab. At last, knee-deep in the calm of the silver-bottomed cove, she put her hands to her face and wept openly as her heart broke and broke and just kept on breaking. She felt the waves nudge the back of her knees and then her thighs with increasing force and frequency; the tide was coming in. Maybe she should just stand here and drown – God knows she deserved to. She heard a soft whimper and felt something solid bump against her legs and opened her eyes, jumping away with a little scream.

Still on her back, and now much calmer because the waves were smaller and rocked her gently, little Asha looked up at her, and sneezed. And then, as a wavelet impolitely slopped water into her open mouth, began coughing and bawling. Some sea goddess had smiled upon them both and sent the baby on her way with a flying kiss; some magic current had swirled the child around before she reached the cutthroat reef and had sent her floating serenely into the mouth of the cove, like a ship gliding into harbour.

Incredulous, Maya lifted her up and thumped her back, and the phlegmatic little toddler stopped coughing and crying after a while and beamed at her. Still trembling, Maya examined the baby from head to foot. She seemed none the worse for wear from her expedition on the high seas. Maya held her close and rocked her.

'Baby!' she whispered, through her tears, 'please don't ever do that again! Don't ever make me murder you like that again. But where's your mom?' It was quite difficult carrying Asha up to the top of the rock, and Maya's arms were aching by the time she reached. She descended carefully too, Asha ever game, chuckling and gurgling in her ear. She carried the baby back, calming her, cuddling her, thumping her on her back to get all the water out of her lungs. By the time she had clambered over Razor Rock 2, Asha seemed to have completely forgotten her recent misadventure and wanted to walk alongside Maya. Her eyes were red-rimmed, her nose ran, her tiny pink hands and feet were as crinkled as the petals of chrysanthemums and she still sneezed and coughed from time to time, but even now she made a determined beeline for the still rock pools that glinted in the sun. But by the time they reached Rock 1, she had asked to be carried and had rested her mop of curls on Maya's shoulders and fallen asleep. Maya wrapped her up in her towelling robe and plodded on, still gulping back the odd escapee sob. It was only when she got off the rocky causeway, that she noticed the hubbub on the beach. People were running frantically up and down, staring out at sea and shouting, others sweeping the waters with binoculars. Someone was charging up the beach towards the fishing village, shouting for boats to be sent out. On the sand, Smita was sitting up in the sand pale as a mushroom, and was having her head bandaged by the resort's medic. At first no one noticed Maya, then someone spotted her and shouted. The crowd turned and stared at her, and the excited babble rose to a crescendo.

'Smita!' Maya called, but in the cacophony of voices who was to hear her? 'Smita!'

Slowly the devastated young mother looked up, her face a shattered death mask. Step by step Maya walked up to her like an apparition from heaven, the baby in her arms. The babble died down and a hush descended and suddenly Maya realized why.

'Smita!' she called, 'she's okay! She's fine!' Maya bent down and kissed the mop of curls and the baby snuggled her face deep into her shoulders. She couldn't get a word in edgeways for a long time after that. A cheer and a roar went up and the crowd – mainly staff and guests at the resort – clustered close, patting her on the back and clapping.

'She's rescued the baby!'

'I've seen her! She runs on the beach every day! What an athlete!'

'Plunged into the waves without a thought to her own safety!'

'Look! Her hands and arms are bleeding! Here miss, the doctor will give first aid!'

'Arre, where are those TV people? This is hot news! Call them, men, call them!'

'What a heroine!'

'She fought the current, men. And it is so strong – it swept the baby right out of her mother's arms!'

'The sea at this time is so dangerous!'

'Here she is, Smita,' Maya said simply, as Asha, awakened by the hullabaloo reached out for her mother's arms. 'She's okay.'

Some ten minutes later (as the crowd increased – most of the fishing village had turned up now), Smita had recovered enough to hand her baby to her parents, who had come down hotfoot, having heard what had happened, accompanied by an instant! crew from *Instantnews!* Now she just broke down completely as she took Maya into her arms, sobbing, 'Thank you, thank you! Oh thank you!' as pretty young Ruchika Sharma stuck a mike in her face and the camera whirred. (The poor girl was close to tears herself.)

'You know,' Smita sobbed, embracing Maya time and again and turning brokenly to the reporter, 'you know Maya told me so many times that she's terrified of being out of her depth and swimming in the sea. But she brought my little Asha back! She brought my Asha back!'

'Is that true, miss? Maya?' the reporter asked Maya, shoving the mike towards her. Maya just nodded dumbly, wiping away her own tears. 'Yes,' she whispered, 'Yes, but…'

They didn't let her get any buts in. 'And so, we have just seen this young girl, Maya what – Sabherwal, out here on holiday, from – Delhi – who's terrified of the sea, plunge in and rescue little Asha, granddaughter of Mr Arvind Baga, the head of *Instantnews!*'

'She said she was more scared of the sea than Asha was!' Smita repeated. She couldn't believe she'd ever see her baby again. The reporter switched the mike back to her.

'If you're feeling better ma'am, could you tell us what happened?' she asked.

'We were playing as usual,' Smita said. 'When this wave came sweeping around and knocked me off my feet! I hit my head on a rock and fell unconscious. When I got up, my baby was gone. Just gone!' She was sobbing again. 'I never thought I'd see her again!' There had hardly been anyone on the beach at the time, and Smita had fallen behind a sandbank, which hid her from view. It was only when she regained consciousness several minutes later that the alarm was raised. By that time, Asha was sailing safely into the sanctuary of the cove, and was bumping into Maya's legs. The mike went back to Maya.

'And Maya, where were you at the time?'

'Er sitting out there ... on those rocks at the end of that third er...islet!'

'Isn't that a dangerous place to go to?'

'Not really!'

'And then what happened.'

'And then,' Maya's voice dropped to a whisper. 'And then I saw Asha. In the sea I mean, floating on her back...'

'And you plunged in and brought her back!' The excited reporter was getting ahead of herself again.

'It... it didn't quite happ...' Overcome, Maya put her hands in her face and sobbed.

'I think the shock is only now beginning to kick in!' Ruchika Sharma remarked wisely. She turned towards the camera. 'So young Maya Sabherwal here, from Delhi, has undoubtedly rescued this baby from the Arabian Sea, and a better example of courage you cannot get. Asha's mother has just told us that Maya was terrified of the sea – yet this brave young girl leapt into the waves with no thoughts for her own safety and brought the baby out! This is Ruchika

Sharma reporting live from Shanbagh Resort for *Instantnews!,* And Ruchika Sharma was looking pretty overwhelmed herself. Who would have imagined that her first live news story would turn out to be like this?

In a daze, they walked back to the resort, and through the corner of her eye, Maya spotted Hari recording the whole tamasha. He came up to her and put his arm around her.

'Congratulations!' he said. 'You're a very, very brave person!'

And suddenly she was the toast of the place. By lunchtime a stream of well-wishers had come to the cottage to congratulate her and had filled it up with flowers. Pankaj Mama and Sadhna Mami had come down too with a gigantic basket of orchids and a massive chocolate cake (as if it were her birthday).

'Wonderful!' Pankaj Mama kept repeating as he hugged her, 'Wonderful! We are so proud of you! I can't wait to ring your Mama and Papa!' But he was canny enough to realize the damage that could have been done to his business had anything happened to Asha. People might think twice before venturing out on a beach where a baby had been taken by the sea. Well the sea had indeed taken a baby, but mercifully – and thanks to his quiet niece – the matter hadn't ended in tragedy, which is what counted ultimately. That's what stuck in people's minds. 'I'm hosting a lunch in your honour in the dining room my dear!' he boomed. Sherry had embraced her and squealed all over her. When she entered the dining room for lunch all the guests rose to their feet and gave her a standing ovation. Sherry squealed and squealed and phoned about a hundred of her friends, with the news.

The gaunt, broody schoolgirl cousin from Delhi had come good. Done herself – and everyone – proud. Knocked their socks off.

Mr and Mrs Baga, both also in tears, embraced her like she were their own daughter and presented her with the most gigantic bouquet of roses and box of chocolates she had ever seen. Smita, with the indefatigable Asha in tow, just hugged her wordlessly, bringing the tears flooding back to both their eyes.

'I'm going to recommend you for the National Award for Bravery, my dear!' Mr Baga said. 'And make damned sure that you get it!'

'Maya! Imagine, you'll be riding on an elephant in the Republic Day parade!' Sherry screamed, clapping her hands.

By the evening two more TV news channels had got wind of the rescue and sent their crews down to interview her. All afternoon the phone had rung relentlessly as reporters from local as well as national dailies wished to speak to her. And Maya knew now, it was far too late to change her story in any way. It gnawed at her like a wound that would not heal, but she was helpless to do anything about it now. And also, she was beginning to enjoy the attention being showered upon her by all and sundry. For the first time in her life, she was the centre of universe! Sherry had rung up her parents – still in Bombay – and her mother, typically first misheard.

'But how can Asha rescue Maya from the sea?' Mrs Sabherwal bellowed down a bad line. 'She's just a baby, no!'

'Auntie no! Maya dived in and pulled the baby out of the sea!'

'But how can that be? Maya is terrified of the water!'

'Pinkie Auntie, just tune into *Instantnews!* She's on the national network. She's a national heroine! Here speak to her!'

'Hi, Mama,' Maya whispered, clutching the receiver as if it were the only friend she had left in the world.

'Maya! But you're so scared of the water! How did you go swimming and rescue Asha?'

'It… just happened, Mama. It just happened!'

'Good girl, Maya!' her father boomed. 'Wonderful!'

'Jay will be so proud when he hears!' her mother said, back on the line.

And somehow, Maya was just a little glad that Yash had not rung up to congratulate her. Maybe he had just not heard about it. Or – no – maybe he had just forgotten her already…

So this, Maya thought, this is how it feels to be like Jay! To be fussed and lorded over all the time! To be treated like a celebrity.

People looked at you with respect and awe in their eyes. They didn't run their leery eyes up and down you, and pronounce you gaunt and broody. Well, she could live with it! That night, again in the dining room, she had had to sign autographs on menu cards and paper napkins and have her photograph taken with several of the resort's guests. At the end, the guests crowded around her and boisterously sang, 'For she's a jolly good fellow!' making her blush.

Earlier that evening a buzz had gone round the resort. Rumour had it that the BBC and maybe CNN were sending down teams to interview her! Somehow, this gaunt broody runner from Delhi, with her grave troubled eyes had caught the imagination of the public. It was probably due to what Smita had said and repeated during her first interview – about how Maya had told her earlier that she was more terrified of the sea than even little Asha – and yet had plunged in heedlessly and rescued the baby. This was no crack long-distance swimmer – but just a schoolgirl who got panic attacks when she couldn't feel the bottom of a pool. And yet… And the phone would simply not stop ringing. Complete strangers were calling up and congratulating her, some even breaking down on the phone.

Sherry went ballistic in her cupboard, pulling out numerous outfits she thought Maya ought to wear for her interviews.

'Imagine! The BBC! And CNN! You'll be in Hollywood next, darling!' (Logic was never a strong point with Sherry.) She winked at Maya. 'Hey, has your little boyfriend rung you up yet to congratulate you?' she asked.

'I've told you he's not my boyfriend. And he probably doesn't know about it yet!'

'Darling the whole world knows! Don't worry, he'll call eventually – they all do in the end!'

'But first,' said Hari who had slipped into Sherry's room, where they had gone 'for a gossip' after dinner, 'before you leave, I'd like to have a word with you and show you something!' He was talking in what Maya privately called his 'priest's voice'. In his nostril, the plug of snot glimmered. Well, maybe she thought, he's going to apologize after all – for all that groping and what had happened at the party. You did not fool around with national heroines after all.

And when Sherry got involved in a long tele-conference with Arunda and Donny about her mermaid takes, he escorted her to his room.

'Don't worry,' he smiled holding up his hands in a gesture of mock surrender. 'It's just something I want you to talk to you about and see.' He sat down by his computer and set it going.

'You know,' he said, 'Papa's got this resort business going and expects me to take it over eventually!' He grimaced. Oh god, she thought, not the true confessions of Harishchand, please! 'But I'm not cut out for it. He charges the people who stay here exorbitant sums and calls them his guests! They're his clients, nothing else. I don't see why anyone ought to pay Rs 5000 and more to spend a night here.'

'Well, I suppose it's not exactly an ashram. Besides if there are people willing to pay that much, that's their lookout. They obviously think they're getting their money's worth!'

'But it's such a worthless way of spending your life! Smiling at and being gratuitous to thugs and blackmarketeers and people who have never paid taxes in their lives and who have come here for dirty weekends. I want to do something more meaningful with my life. I'm after the truth! And anyway, Papa doesn't think I can do anything properly.'

'Oh,' but she was wondering where this conversation was going. Had Hari simply drunk more beer than he ought to have and had become garrulous as a result? He was shaking his head. 'But it's not so simple Maya, it's not so simple. Even when you find the truth you can get yourself in a jam.'

'Oh, what do you mean?' she asked, in spite of herself.

'This,' he said, 'now watch!' He slipped a CD from a case into the computer.

He'd got it all: her mooning about in the cove looking lovelorn and a bit silly. Climbing over the rocks to the edge. Staring out at sea. He'd zoomed in now, and even caught the stiffening of her shoulders as she spotted Asha. Then, some blurry movement over the sea as the camera searched for Asha – and then maximum zoom on the baby and her bright orange floaters.

Herself; reaching out imploringly and then putting one foot gingerly into the sea and withdrawing it. Lowering herself in and panicking as the waves rocked her off her feet, the first time. Then clambering up trembling and crawling her way back over the rocks like a reptile with a broken back. Standing in the cove, her hands in front of her face, weeping because of her cowardice and the murder she had just committed. As behind her, borne on the breath of some guardian angel, the baby floated in safe and serene and bumped into her legs, whimpering.

'The truth!' said Hari softly. 'Now you know why I'm in a jam!' He smiled and raised an eyebrow. 'Though I think the BBC and CNN would be interested in the truth, don't you? In seeing this footage...' And added to himself, 'though I wonder who will pay more for an exclusive!'

'Hari!' her voice came out in a whisper. 'Hari… you can't show them this. Please!'

'It's the truth!' he said in that tone that made her sick. 'It's the truth and it must get out, Maya!' He gave her a quizzical look. 'What do you think?'

'But, but…,' she said, 'I tried… I tried and fell in… you haven't shown that…'

'Really? I must have somehow missed it. I could hardly hold the camera steady. Too bad!'

She was white as she whispered the words. 'Hari, please! What do you want?'

'I thought we can discuss it. Tomorrow morning at that cove you like so much. About 10 a.m. High tide's at around 11.30. Meet you there and we'll talk about it. Wear your swimsuit and bring plenty of sunscreen.'

He'd plunged his knife in and twisted it good.

She rescued the baby they said
Not knowing that really she'd fled
Terrified of the waves
But a heroine so brave
Who wished she really were dead

There was a heroine called Maya
Who was such a convincing liar
She left the baby to drown
But became talk of the town
To such great heights she did aspire!

9

She slept badly that night, tossing and turning and dreaming of being stranded on sandy islets as the waves came rushing towards her to consume her or the sand beneath her turned to jelly. She was in the water, flat on her back and then sinking, somersaulting, tumbling, in a welter of blue and silver, going deeper and never, never touching the bottom no matter how much she stretched her toes. And Hari, smiling at her in his horrible saintly way, and throwing discs into the sea, only he seemed to have a never-ending supply of them. She awoke with a jerk and a small scream, trembling and sweating. On the sofa-cum-bed nearby, Maria slept on peacefully.

Her ankle was much better the next morning, and though she didn't want to risk running, she was able to walk on the beach without any discomfort. She set off on a long walk, hoping it would lighten the boulder that appeared to have settled permanently in her stomach and the sense of dread that loomed just over the horizon. As she approached the fishing village at the far end, her little shell-selling friend, accompanied by a whole gaggle of friends came running out in delight and grabbed her hand possessively.

'Madam, heroine! My customer!' he said, 'do not disturb her, hut, hut!' And waved his friends away like so many flies. She smiled and asked.

'Well what have you got for me today? As usual I've forgotten to bring any money!'

'Never mind, you come!' he said and led her into the village. The boats were drawing in again, and this time, the fisher-folk stopped their work and surrounded her with dazzling smiles. The women especially, crowded around her and patted her on the back, and Maya was astonished to see that some were wiping their eyes with their sari.

The word had got around – this strange girl who ran on the sand every morning, but who it was said could hardly swim herself – had plunged into the sea and rescued a drowning child. It didn't matter to them that it had been the grandchild of a lala or seth or television tycoon – it was a child, a baby, and that was enough. They smiled and talked volubly, some telling her about the children and men they had lost to the sea, others of small and big victories they had snatched from it. They plied her with tea and soggy biscuits and asked if she would like a cold drink.

'Wait!' her little salesman ordered as she prepared to leave, almost in tears. 'Not go, yet, please!' He vanished into one of the tin-roofed huts and emerged holding a huge circular biscuit tin clutched to his chest. A pink satin ribbon with a bow was tied around it. 'For you!' he said simply, thrusting it at her. They crowded around her now, the men flashing big grins, the women still patting her on her back and nodding, the children jumping up and down with ill-concealed excitement. Whatever it was Maya knew it was from the whole village.

The tin was unexpectedly heavy and had a gaudy picture of a prince and princess descending a royal red-carpeted staircase – now pitted and spotted with rust.

'Open!' her friend demanded. 'Open now!'

She undid the ribbon and opened the box.

'But… but… but this is like a treasure chest!' she whispered, staring at the stunning array of shells packed tight in the box gleaming up at her like jewels.

'Madam like shells?' her friend asked anxiously, because there was a distinctly fishy odour emerging from the box.

Maya nodded. 'They're exquisite! But…' But she knew she could not refuse the undeserved gift. She bent her head to hide her tears and stared at them, still stunned.

There were cowries, in chocolate and gold, delicate pink and magenta, ivory white, looking freshly lacquered, fan-shaped scallops and cockles beautifully ribbed, razor-edged butterfly-like shells, delicately hinged at the centre in pearl pink and mauve and iridescent green. And others with whorls and spires and ice-cream cone spirals, worked with exquisite patterns in gold, orange, maroon, purple, ochre and black. Some glowed with the luster of pearls, others were matte finished.

'And these also,' her friend said, 'these not fitting into box!' And handed her two more massive conches. 'Now you can hear sea with both ears at same time!' he pointed out. She was in tears when she left, clutching her undeserved bounty; it felt so good and yet she felt so utterly horrible. It was a twisted perverted nightmare that just got worse. She went back to the cottage and laid the shells out on the sit out.

'Dry them properly,' Maria instructed her. 'Or they will stink the place out and your Mama will not let you keep them.'

'Just look at them,' Maya said slowly being drawn back by the magic of the box, 'this one looks like the headgear of a bishop, and this one like a wizard's hat – and this one like some maharaja's turban! And just look at this – like the helmet of a Viking warrior!' There were others that looked like miniature minarets and onion domes and the fantastic castle towers of Disney World, and some that were just petrified flowers… How did they get to become so beautiful and perfect and what magic artist carved and worked those intricate, delicate patterns on them? She bent low over them, her facing clearing for the first time that morning, and Maria cocked an eyebrow and smiled.

Of course, it was too good to last, and the glow dimmed from her smoky eyes all too soon. Now, now there was Hari to contend with…

He was already there when she dragged herself to Razor Rock 3 and peered down fearfully at that little cove, where light years ago she had unashamedly taken Yash into her arms. He was pacing up and down the little beach, his hands clasped behind his back, looking as if he were in deep thought. He was in baggy purple trunks, a towel thrown over his pale body. His legs were the colour of white butter. It made her slightly sick just to look at him; he was like some horrible pulsating maggot. Her face set, she clambered down the rocks, not daring to glance at the ledge where she had been with Yash as she passed it. He looked up as she stepped cautiously on to the sand and snuck a glance at his watch.

'Ah, Maya, hi! Great right on time. Come on, come on!'

He waited until she was standing in front of him her eyes staring fixedly over his shoulder. She'd wrapped her towelling robe snugly around her, but it was not going to give her much protection. He smiled, his pale transparent eyes widening in concern.

'Relax, you're much too tense!'

She glanced around, but saw no sign of the hateful camcorder. Perhaps he'd forgotten to bring it. 'What do you want, Hari?' she asked dully, wishing to get it over with quickly, but knowing that this was just the beginning. He put his arm around her and smiled.

'First, I want you to relax. Come, let me help you get this off.' And undid her girdle. She took off her robe before he could and flushed. 'Hari, please…'

'Now, I just want to talk to you…' he said, putting an arm around her shoulder and making her flinch. 'This is such a lovely little private beach, don't you think.'

'About what? What do you want to talk about?'

'About what happened yesterday, with little Asha! I saw you Maya, and I have nothing but admiration for the way you tried to fight your fear. And there was nothing wrong about going back – you simply panicked – and I think we're all entitled to panic at least once in our lives, don't you!' He drew her closer now as she tensed, elder brotherly like. 'There was nothing to be ashamed about!'

'Then, what?' For a fraction of a second hope flickered. Maybe…

'But what I couldn't understand was what happened later… When you got back to the beach and told them you swam out in the sea and rescued little Asha…' He tried looking and sounding pained and puzzled as if she had betrayed a great trust he had reposed in her.

'Hari, I never said that! They just assumed…'

'And you let them assume it. You should have corrected them then and there! That would have been the right thing to do!' He sounded like a damn priest again.

'Things… things just went out of control… there were so many people… the noise.' But it was hopeless; she knew she had blundered – and badly. She could have taken the mike from that reporter woman and clearly announced to the world what had really happened. That she, Maya Sabherwal had chickened out and that little Asha had been saved by some guardian angel of the sea.

'Maya, you became a heroine under false pretenses,' he said holding her hand and squeezing it, gazing deep into her eyes, looking betrayed.

'Hari… Hari, please wipe your nose first!' she said, turning away, almost retching.

He flushed. 'Look,' he said, 'this is as hard for me as it is for you. I have got what happened on disc, as you saw, and now am in a dilemma as to what to do about it. I don't want you to be hurt and yet the truth should not be suppressed.'

'So what do you want to do Hari?' she whispered wishing he would come to the point and stop playing her out on the line.

'You see, Maya if this disc were to be released, it would hurt you yes. But have you thought of what it would do to Pinkie Auntie? And to you father and to Vish? Not to mention Papa and Mama? All of us here! And Smita and Arvind Uncle – it would devastate her and he'd be made a laughing stock of by the world media!'

'So you are not going to release it?' she asked.

'It's not as easy as that Maya. I have my duty to the truth. Mahatma Gandhi said, "there is no religion greater than the truth," did you know that? If I am to become anything as an investigative journalist I cannot ignore that! I find my whole life hinges on the decision I take now.'

'Which is what, Hari?'

'I need time to think about it,' he said, and plunged his knife in deep. He licked his lips, 'and I think you can help me think...'

'How?' she whispered, the horror as heavy as lead.

'By taking your swimsuit off for me, Maya!' he said softly. 'I promise I won't touch you!' Yet, but he never said that aloud.

'M... my swimsuit... Hari please!'

'I think you need to put on some sunscreen lotion,' he said sotto voce. 'I'd hate it if you got sunburned! You tan so beautifully. Golden brown. Even Sherry's envious.'

'Sun... sunburned?'

'Okay,' he said holding up his hands, his breath coming in shallow gulps. 'We can do it like this... You get into the water there and take off your swimsuit. And then rise and walk slowly out... like a mermaid!'

'You're sick!'

'And I have the disc! Go on Maya, we can't be here all day. Someone might come looking for us!'

'I can't do it Hari...' she sobbed. 'Please, stop this!'

'You didn't mind doing it with your midget boyfriend, did you?' he said with soft viciousness, the barb hitting home. She flinched and stared at him in horror. How the hell did he know? But if he had seen her and Yash he would have started all this much earlier. 'Neha told me you had love bites on your breast!' he said guilelessly. 'I want to see them!' He glanced at his watch. 'Come on, Maya be a sweet girl now. Just for me... Take off your swimsuit!'

Blindly she waded into the water, chest high, afraid of the gentle swells that threatened to lift her off her feet. She shut her eyes. 'Okay,' she thought desperately, 'it's really Yash who is there, waiting for me...'

Of course, it didn't work. For a moment, defiance flared. Maybe she should tell him to do what he liked with the disc. Let the world see! Maya Sabherwal – heroine one day, zeroine the next. Coward and liar! But... but Yash! There was also Yash! It would... she couldn't imagine what it would do to him...

'Right,' Hari called. 'No deeper! Now turn around...'

Like an automation she turned around to face the little beach. Her hands slipped up to her swimsuit straps and she lowered them off her shoulders.

'Walk forward,' he called hoarsely. 'Come into the shallows and take it off completely!'

She did as she was told and dared not to see what he was doing with his hands.

'Okay,' he gasped at last, his face bright red. 'You can get dressed now!'

And as they walked back, he put in yet another knife. 'Really Maya, I don't know why you are so upset. As I told you that night – be grateful for small mercies!' And added, musingly, more to himself. 'Next time, I'm thinking of bringing the camcorder along! So get a nice tan!'

'Next time?' So there was to be a next time. And a time after that... for another whole month, maybe...

Sitting in his bedroom the previous night Hari had plotted his strategy in diabolical detail.

'Step by step,' he told himself, 'slowly, slowly catch the monkey!'

First he would simply ask her to take her swimsuit off and see how she reacted. No camera, no touching. Now the camera – that could be a tricky proposition – a double-edged sword really. He could film her naked all right, but really wouldn't be able to use it against her, unlike the stuff he already had. If his father came to know that he had been filming her – he'd be flayed alive. Put that sort of stuff on the web and you could be sure someone would send a clip to his parents. So he'd have to keep it only to himself – well that would be nice for when she went away… Maybe at a later stage then. As for touching her… He'd groped her in the dark but was afraid of touching her openly in broad daylight. What if she screamed 'rape!' and brought everyone on the beach running? Then he slapped his plump thighs and grinned. That small alcove in Little Rock! It would be perfect. He'd ask her to fold her clothes neatly beside his – if anyone caught them – there would be trouble of course, but not to the extent of it being rape (technically it could have been because Maya was under eighteen, but he didn't know that) – the young naughty couple had obviously done this consentingly. Besides, in that alcove no one could possibly hear anything. Right, get there with her at a time when the tide was just coming in and they'd be 'stranded' there for at least five hours! Five hours with Maya in that private little alcove, with the sea all around them… He was dribbling and had to wipe his nose quickly.

The first morning had gone off perfectly to plan. She had been cooperative and as docile as a sheep. He turned to her now, and smiled, 'I think we could meet again tomorrow don't you think?' he said, risking a quick squeeze. She flinched and jerked away.

And so, for the next three days, Maya walked to Razor Rock 3 at the time Hari had stipulated, like she was going for her execution. And revelling in his power, Hari was getting bolder by the day. Even Sherry, with her head in the clouds noticed.

'What's up bro?' she asked him eyeing him up and down. 'Why the sudden swagger in your step? Why are you suddenly strutting around like the cock of the rock?' And Sherry had even noticed the change in Maya. She clicked her tongue. 'I hope poor Maya is not sickening for something. She's looking so gaunt and broody these days – Arunda was right really!'

Hari shrugged. 'Must be some girl thing or she's missing her mother!' he said.

'Or her little boyfriend! Maybe she's got it worse than we know! Maybe he's dumped her!'

'That pipsqueak!' Hari muttered, wondering what the hell Maya had seen in him. That morning he had forced her to put sunscreen on his back and chest – with her swimsuit off. Alas he hadn't lasted two minutes and it was a pity that she was sick on the sand. Tomorrow it would be his turn to put sunscreen on her – everywhere!

'Hari, you're dribbling!' Sherry exclaimed staring at him. She grinned knowingly. 'Ah, fantasizing about Neha in that bikini of hers, I'll bet!'

'Shut up, Sherry!'

'Well, if I were you I would,' she went on. 'Though it hardly leaves anything to the imagination!'

He ignored her. Maybe… maybe he should ask – no order – Maya to buy herself a bikini too…

And for Maya, there seemed no end to the horror of these days. Maria eyed the dark rings around her eyes, and her gaunt expression with increasing concern.

'You must eat well!' she admonished as Maya pushed her plate away, yet again. 'What will your mummy say when she gets back. That I have starved you! Look at you! Becoming like a stick insect!' And then, more gently, 'are you having a problem?'

'No, Maria thanks. I'm fine. Just a bit tired that's all. I'll be all right!'

Smita and Asha had stopped coming out on the beach after the baby's misadventure. But a day after Hari had begun his blackmailing, Smita had rung Maya up and asked her over.

'Asha's fretting and cranky because we don't go out to the beach anymore,' she said. 'She'll be happy to see you. And so will I!'

'Okay, Smita! I'll be happy to come over!'

It was a relief to be with Smita and Asha again, even though there was that leaden boulder in the pit of her stomach, every time she looked at them. At least Asha was safe! Suppose… suppose she had not been at the cove that morning… No one would ever have known that the baby was there and soon the rising tide would have claimed her. So, yes, she had saved the little girl's life – not heroically perhaps, but technically certainly. So perhaps she ought not to berate herself like she was doing and feel like such a creep.

The poison dart devil let fly its barb: Bottom line Maya, you are still a coward. You left the baby to its fate – to drown and die – and slunk back!

And what a price I'm paying for it, she gulped. What a price!

She walked over to the Baga's palatial villa next door. The impressive watchman at the gate snapped to attention and gave her a smart salute, smiling broadly. She was the girl who had rescued little Asha. She was welcomed royally, and Smita's mother embraced her with tears in her eyes. 'Come, my dear,' she said. 'Smita and Asha will be so glad to see you!'

But Smita's eyes widened when she saw Maya.

'What's the matter, Maya? You're looking so pale and pulled down! You feeling okay?'

'I'm fine, Smita. Hi Asha!' She picked up the little girl and kissed her. 'And how are you, Smita?' she asked.

'Still recovering from the shock,' Smita said. 'I still get nightmares about what happened!'

'So do I!' Maya admitted truthfully. She was wondering if she ought to tell Smita the truth about what had happened. Maybe she would understand. Even if the secret went no further, and Hari went on with his blackmail, at least it would give her someone she could talk to. But Smita couldn't possibly keep quiet. Her father was the boss of '*Instantnews*!' and was recommending her for a bravery award! So that option was out.

'Asha must be missing the beach,' she said. 'I haven't seen you both there since the accident.'

'I'm petrified of the sea now,' Smita said. 'And Papa and everyone at home refuses to let us go out. Only Asha frets a lot. It's stupid really – to have this lovely villa on the beach and not be able to go out on it.'

'I suppose after a while, you will forget and go back to it,' she said, wishing she could deal with her own fears in the same way. 'I don't think you'd be able to keep a water baby like Asha out of the sea for long. You know… everyone's been so incredibly sweet to me. The people of the fishing village gifted me this humongous box of the most beautiful shells I've ever seen. I don't know the names of most of them, or where they came from, but they're exquisite. I'll bring them along the next time.'

'Maya, what's wrong?' Smita was more observant than she had been given credit for. 'Are you sure you're all right? Not coming down with anything? There's this dull look in your eye…'

And tears now, that welled up without warning.

'Hey, what's the matter Maya?'

She wiped her eyes and gulped. She couldn't tell Smita about the fake rescue she had pulled off – but she could tell her about Yash – at least some part of it.

'I'm stupid really… I think I have a crush on a boy…'

Smita smiled with relief. 'One of Sherry's friends down from Bombay?' she asked. 'They don't seem to be your type though.'

'No, not them! A boy I met here – well he's gone now.'

Smita crinkled her eyebrows. 'Not that little fellow in the red swimming trunks who was running around on the beach a few days ago? I did see the two of you together.'

The look on Maya's face told her everything.

'I know… I know he's awfully young,' Maya went on defensively, but he was Yash and it didn't matter how old or young he was. He was Yash.

'And now you're missing him and mooning about all day pining for him?'

Ah, if it had only been just that.

'We didn't… we didn't break up or anything like that… Smita is it okay to… to have a… crush on someone so much younger? Or is something wrong with me?' And of course it wasn't just a silly little crush – it was far more secret and precious than that.

'No one knows for sure what is okay and what is not in these matters,' Smita said her eyes twinkling, patting her hand. 'It just happens. So I can't say anything on that. But you're lucky. You still… like each other you can keep in touch… Of course it might just fade away quietly in time and leave you with a warm and sweet memory…'

She spent the rest of that day with Smita and Asha, and felt much better than she had for days. At last she got up to leave.

'Just a minute Maya,' Smita said, 'there's something I want you to have.'

She disappeared into an adjoining room and emerged after a few minutes carrying a heavy gift-wrapped package. Oh no, not again, not another undeserved gift.

'No… I… I… please…!'

'Just take it Maya, it's from Asha and me!'

'What is it?'

'Open it and see,' Smita smiled.

It was a huge, glossy book, *An Encyclopedia of Shells of the World's Oceans and Reefs*. Exquisitely illustrated. Breathlessly, Maya leafed through it, recognizing with delight some of the shells she had in her collection.

'Thank you,' she said, 'thanks so much! This is fabulous!'

'It was providence that the book was lying here all this while,' Smita said smiling. I had been wondering what to give you and then you mentioned shells and well, everything just clicked!'

But of course, that devil's voice had to spoil things a bit, by whispering, 'ill gotten gains, Maya, more ill-gotten gains, eh!' And another little devil had begun asking her why that little idiot Yash had not bothered to ring her up so far. Surely he would have heard the news by now. Had he forgotten to take the resort's number – no but his parents would have had it – or had he just forgotten about her the moment he had driven out of the resort's gates, period… as he did all his other friends?

She would have been over the moon had she known how wrong she was.

'I don't understand you guys, I just don't understand you guys!' Yash exclaimed glumly from the back of the car as they drove out of Shanbagh Resort, early that morning, while Maya slept on fitfully after the disastrous party night. He shook his head exasperatedly. 'You can't stay in one place for more than half an hour at a time!'

'What on earth are you talking about now?' his mother asked sleepily.

'I tell you, you guys have the attention span of monkeys!'

His mother yawned and opened her eyes. Had there been the slightest hint of tears in Yash's voice?

'What's the matter now, Yash? What's bothering you?'

'I mean, just look at us! Like a band of roving gypsies! Like… like we're on the run from cops or the mafia! We come to India to settle down, we find this beautiful place by the ocean, and what do you do? Start packing almost before you've finished unpacking!'

Mrs Ahuja sighed. They had travelled rather a lot in the last five or six years and it had had its effect on Yash. Perhaps they ought to have put him into boarding school, though her husband had been dead against it, based on his own experiences as a boy.

'I mean…' Yash went on, 'I can't talk to anyone for more than ten minutes without saying, "sorry I got to go – we're leaving town!"'

'Yash, you do exaggerate! But think of how lucky you are! You've already seen more places and cities than most people do in a lifetime!'

'Lucky? Lucky? I really like that!'

'What's bothering you Yash?'

'For once, why can't we stay put in one place for a while? Like here!'

'You like the place? Well, we can always come back here again. But there are so many other wonderful places to see. And anyway, we'll soon have to decide where we want to live permanently.'

'Hah! Do you know I've never actually seen most of my friends? They're just names and pictures on the net!'

'Well,' said Mrs Ahuja smiling, 'you did make friends with that nice girl here – what was her name – Maya – didn't you?'

Privately Mrs Ahuja had wondered how that tall pleasant girl had tolerated her hellion son for so long, remembering the innumerable complaints she'd faced by the mothers of children – and especially girls – that Yash had grossed out with some childish prank. As they drove into Calangute, the tirade continued. He looked around him appalled.

'You mean… you mean… this is Goa? The world-famous Goa? It's a dump! Just look at all the rubbish – and so many people!'

They weren't so many people really because it was off season, but yes, compared to the peace and quiet of Shanbagh, it was crowded and cluttered and noisy.

'And so many foreigners!' Yash complained. 'We've come all the way to India to see Indians, not foreigners!'

'Yash, just what are you going on about?' his mother asked exasperated as they drove into the portico of a rather plush hotel to be greeted by a doorman seven feet tall and in a turban with tassels.

'And look at this hotel! It looks like you have to wear a tuxedo even for bed tea in this place!'

It was nonsense of course, (Maya had been right, he did talk a lot of nonsense) but again there was a grain of truth in what he had said. Compared to the easygoing and friendly Shanbagh Resort, this place was a trifle stiff, even if the staff did go around in shorts and bush shirts and smiled rather a lot. There was an indefinable quality missing – a quality that made the Shanbagh Resort forget that you were not at home. In this place, shorts and bush shirts and even the smiles were uniforms; at Shanbagh they was simply what you wore because it was hot and normal.

He had strutted around the swimming pool glancing disdainfully at the girls sunning themselves around it.

Hah! He didn't have to look at them anymore. He didn't have to think about them anymore. He didn't have to think what they were thinking (if such girls could think at all, he snorted) about him anymore as he walked past them, sticking his chest out. He had Maya!

'Just look at them!' he snorted at his father. 'Lying around all day like crocodiles at a watering hole!'

His parents exchanged glances. 'I think we'd better go back in,' his mother said. 'You're beginning to overheat!'

She was right, because just thinking of Maya had caused alarming movement in his shorts and he had to thrust his T-shirt down hurriedly. 'I'm fine,' he said stuffing a handful of chips in his mouth and putting the bag on his lap.

'Coming for a swim?' his father asked, as his parents got up. 'We're going for a dip!'

'We come to the beach and you swim in a pool!' was his scathing comment.

He sat back in the lounger and thought about Maya. Was she making up any more crackpot limericks? Ah, but she had said they only came when something happened or when she was upset and he didn't want her to be upset, but then she wouldn't make up any limericks, so maybe she should be a little upset every now and then, maybe she was upset right now because he was not there and had not been able to go to that party with her… But she was the only girl in the whole world who had ever – ever – shown interest in his warships and sea battle games – and joined them with such enthusiasm. Definitely the only girl in the whole wide world who hadn't thought he was a monstrous little creep too big for his boots who played nasty pranks on them. And certainly the only girl – probably in the whole universe – no in all the universes there were – who would ever take him into her most secret and precious places and make him explode there like some incredible fusion bomb. (Even if there were others who were keen to, and who knew there were probably hundreds he didn't know about, he would refuse to go along with them anyway!) And she was seventeen! Seventeen! So she must know what she was doing – even if he didn't quite. Some chick she was! No, not chick, she was too good for that – what a cheap lousy word that was! She was… she was… well, Maya. And he wanted to be naked and in her arms, forever and ever and ever. Of course she would be likewise and oh damn, oh damn, oh damn!

Twenty minutes later he was ready to work on his parents again as they stepped out of the glinting blue pool.

'Tourism,' he declared seriously looking around witheringly, 'has absolutely ruined this place! There must be just a few places left like Shanbagh Resorts, and we of course had to leave that and come here! Really!'

And the following night, in their room, Mr and Mrs Ahuja caught the late night news and watched Ruchika Sharma of 'Instantnews!' interview a sobbing Smita – and then Maya about the dramatic rescue of little Asha.

Yash, who had insisted on watching Rocky III till then, was fast asleep in the small adjoining room (thrown in free as an off-season package).

'Isn't that the girl – Maya – who drove down with us from Bombay with her mother and who Yash made friends with?' Mr Ahuja asked. 'We'd better tell him! He'd be thrilled! His girlfriend is a heroine!'

'Don't wake him!' his mother said. 'He'd just get too excited to sleep.' She pursed her eyebrows. 'Girlfriend did you say?' She smiled slowly. 'You just may be more right than you think, dear. Yash did mention her a lot and hang around with her on the beach. Oh, so that's what the little devil has been playing at!'

'What?'

'You know, this anti-Goa tirade, and complaints about too many tourists and so on. He wants us to go back there of course, because she's still there!'

'She looks a little old for him,' her husband commented doubtfully. 'Girls of her age usually don't make friends with fellows his size.'

'Girls of any age don't seem to!' Mrs Ahuja said dolefully, remembering again the hordes of infuriated mothers who had come knocking or her doors, or that had rung up at all odd hours with horror stories. A thoughtful look entered her eyes.

'You know what…' she said slowly. 'His birthday is coming up in a few days…'

But of course, like all infuriating parents they clean forgot to tell him about the news bulletin the next morning. And when he did get to know, and charged for the phone, it was all coming to a head for Maya.

10

To Sherry's continuing mystification the swagger in Hari's step became cockier by the day and she had even started wondering about his long disappearances from the resort and its grounds. Poor Maya on the other hand really seemed to be missing her little midget boyfriend badly – there was a dead look in her eyes and she moved listlessly, with none of her usual natural grace; she too disappeared for long hours, probably mooning on the beach somewhere Sherry thought, poor kid. Sherry didn't put two and two together, but that was because (like Maya) she had an aversion to mathematics and logic was never her strong point. But she was determined to get to the bottom of what she called 'Hari's infatuation with female or females unknown, probably Neha', though her plans were temporarily thwarted by her own modelling career, which was showing signs of taking off nicely in the near future. As for Hari, revelling in his power over Maya, these were days of triumph and vindication and he relished the way his plans were materializing into action in just the way he envisaged. It wasn't smooth sailing all the way, because Maya was such a frozen bitch sometimes, but he just loved the sword he dangled over her and pricked her with from time to time.

'I don't understand why you are making this so difficult for yourself Maya,' he said, sounding pained and hurt, as he ran his hands over her frozen body. 'We can have such a good time together.' But her eyes had glazed over and she shrivelled at his touch.

'Hari, why are you doing this?' she whispered for the thousandth time. 'Please, why are you doing this to me?' He gave no answer, just shifted closer his hands all over her body, grunting and breathing heavily all over her.

'It's because you can't find anyone else to do this with, isn't it?' she flared with a sudden spurt of anger. 'Your precious friends from Bombay won't let you touch them – not even Neha, and you don't have any hold over them. She can't stand you, can she – God Hari you're pathetic. You need help!'

'Ah, and just look who's talking Maya!' he shot back unctuous as always. 'Look at yourself! You've flunked in class; you've been deemed broody and gaunt by one of the leading ad gurus in the country; you chase little boys behind the rocks; you've become a national heroine on false pretexts because you wanted your fifteen seconds of fame; you're jealous of your baby brother… want me to go on? That is a list of achievements!' He bent over her, his face so close she had to shut her eyes and stop breathing. 'As I told you Maya, be grateful for small mercies, be grateful for small mercies. One day, you will look back on this with longing and regret…'

She should have raked his face with her nails
And slapped him till he quivered and quailed
But she daren't take the risk
Because he had the disc
So she meekly gave up and turned tail!

'How long are you going to continue doing this?' she whispered. 'I can't take it any longer!'

'Maya, you'll have to take it as long as I want, don't you think…' He smiled and leaned over her. 'You see I've thought this through. If you think that people or the media will lose interest in the story after a while, you'd better think again. Think of how sensational the new revelations will be! I can just see the headlines! 'Jealous Schoolgirl Claims Bravery Award Under False Pretexts!' 'Sea Rescue That

Never Was!' 'Failed Schoolgirl Lies About Rescue At Sea!' And if I'm asked why I took so long to release the disc to the media I'll tell them because I was fighting a huge battle with my conscience. Do I protect you and the family, or the truth? Oh God, why give me this terrible choice in the very first big news story of my career! And so, in the end, I decide, that the truth must be out – at whatever cost. Hence... They'd lap it up! Hire me even, maybe!'

She turned her away and shuddered. She could sense it was coming; he had a definite goal in mind and she knew full well what it was going to be. So far, he had only groped and grasped and ogled and grunted and tried kissing her. She had found an ally in the sand, spreading it over her body after having applied lashings of sunscreen lotion and even oil, so it would stick, so that when he pawed and squeezed and tried kissing her, it would chafe and get into his mouth and grit on his teeth.

'I'm going to have you coach you how to make it nice for both myself and you!' he said. 'Okay, put your arms around me... Come on now, Maya be a sweet girl!' But here too she found a counter lever. Whatever it was, whatever he wanted and demanded, she would not cooperate. She just froze up, stone cold and good as dead, except for the occasional shudder of sheer revulsion. She knew he wouldn't dare airing the disc just because she had been uncooperative and stiff as a mannequin. The disc was his ace, and he had to keep it or else lose his hold over her completely. She knew he'd rather have her uncooperative and stiff than not at all. But she knew he was now getting ready to make his big move. And she was right.

'Guess what, Maya!' he said, laying his head in her lap, making her jerk away involuntarily. 'Guess what! Mama and Papa and Sherry are going to Bombay tomorrow morning – they have to attend a wedding there and Sherry's got another shoot. So we'll be left all on our own here. For three whole days! I was thinking we could try coming here at night. I checked the tide timings – we can get here by midnight; high tide is about 5.30 a.m. So we stay here and watch it come in and get back when it recedes.' His eyes glinted, 'and guess what else. It's a full moon night too! Imagine. It'll be so romantic! And we'll snuggle in a very special place that I want to show you.'

Again, Hari had planned it down to the last little detail – or so he liked to think. He'd take Maya up to the alcove on the small rock, and they'd be 'marooned' by the tide for four or five hours. He was slobbering as he thought what could happen in that time, confined in that space with Maya. There was simply nowhere she could go. Another idea came to him and he thumped his hand in his fist. They'd have plenty of time, so he could spend some of that taking shots of Maya, naked in the moonlight, bathing in the cove, and… and… Yes, it was time he took footage and stills of her – you never knew when this whole thing might end – she might fall ill or have a nervous breakdown or leave, so better have that done with. Involuntarily he slurped in the spittle that had started dripping out of the corners of his mouth.

Maya's heart dropped and kept on dropping. So that was what he had been planning. She clung to one final hope.

'I can't do that!' she said. 'Maria sleeps in the room with me! I can't come!'

But Hari had not planned all this to be fobbed off with Maria.

'Make some excuse. Tell her that you're spending the night with Sherry, so she can stay home. I don't care.' He stared at her. 'You see,' he told her softly, 'if you are not at the Rock tomorrow night, then all you need to do is watch BBC news the next day…'

She lay dispiritedly in bed that afternoon in the cottage, as Maria clucked indignantly over her, wondering what was the matter. Boyfriend trouble, she thought, darkly. At this age it was always boyfriend trouble. That little boyfriend who had given that beautiful ship to her had just dumped her. And that wasn't for her to interfere with. She hoped Mrs Sabherwal would be getting back soon, or else would have to have a word with Mrs Shanbagh. The girl was plainly very unhappy.

'Okay, Maya miss, I'm going now!' she said, having left the little cottage spick and span. 'I'll see you in the evening!'

'Bye Maria.'

She lay back and stared up at the ceiling. Tomorrow night... Tomorrow night he would be all over her, grunting like a buffalo, his hands and mouth swarming all over her body, disgusting her beyond belief. And then the night after that and... when would it end? Would she ever be able to stand anyone's hands touching her after he had finished with her?

Will I ever escape from his clutch?
His swarming slithery touch
He's got me with treachery
No end to his lechery
It's becoming a little too much!

The phone rang, startling her.

'Miss Maya?' came the receptionist's friendly voice over the line.

'Yes?'

'Call for you dear!'

'Maya! Hey, man you're a heroine! Wow! You're all over TV! Mom told me and I saw it and... oh wow!'

'Yash? Oh, Yash...!'

'Hey are you crying? What did I say?'

'Nothing... oh Yash!'

'Just imagine! You plunged into the sea, did battle with the waves and brought the baby out! Man, wish I could have done something like that! But I really miss you, this place is a dump!'

She took a deep breath. 'Yash, Yash, just listen a minute! Please!'

'Hey Maya, what's wrong? You know I've been working on my parents to come back to the resort...'

'Yash! It never... it never happened like... like that....' She blurted at last and gulped down a huge sob. 'It didn't happen!'

'What? What didn't happened?'

'The rescue… Asha's rescue…'

'But it was on TV!'

'I know… but I never really did jump into the sea and rescue her. She was… she was washed into our little cove where I was… I just picked her up and brought her back!'

For a moment there was silence. 'You mean…'

'It's worse Yash,' she said, letting the dam burst. 'I… saw her floating in the sea, and I did… did try to get into the water… but the waves were too deep and rough and I got scared and came back. And then there she was suddenly bumping my legs in the cove…' She was weeping now. 'Oh Yash!'

'You mean…?' There was a silence. Awestruck, wonderstruck, thunderstruck! And horrorstruck she thought dully, most of all horrorstruck.

'Wheeeohweee! Man oh man. Maya you are just too much!' He was whooping and whistling down the line so loud she had to hold the receiver away. 'You… you…' He was jumping up and down thumping his hands into his fists.

'What's the matter, are you okay Yash?' she asked wondering if she had pushed him over the edge. But his reaction had brought just the tiniest twitches of a smile to the corners of her mouth.

'Man oh man! You mean you took all those fat cat TV fellows for a ride? You took the whole big shooting match for a ride! Getting interviewed and all that! Maya I wish I were there! Getting your pictures in all the papers! You must be having a ball! Oh my God!' And only Yash could have seen it from that (slightly crooked) viewpoint she thought, her heart lurching. Only Yash.

'I swear I didn't tell them that I'd jumped in and brought Asha out. I didn't, they just assumed I had!'

'That's their problem then!'

'And now the BBC might be interviewing me…'

'The BBC? Wow! Great! Too much!'

'Yash, that's not the horrible part…'

'Horrible? What horrible part?'

She took a deep breath. 'You know Hari? My cousin. He shot what really happened on his camera – he showed me. It's awful! And he says he's going to give it to the BBC…'

'What?' Another silence. Now horrorstruck. 'The bloody asshole… Sorry I shouldn't have said that word in your hearing!' But the fizz had gone out of his voice; he was realizing the implications that it might have for her. 'Oh, no! Can't you… can't you sneak into his room and smash his camera and computer or something? Set his house on fire?'

'Yash, sweetie there's more. It gets worse. He says he'll release the disc if I don't go with him to the Rock tomorrow night… Everyone else is away…. He's planned this all out…'

'Hang on Maya, I'm coming!' he yelled, 'I'll… I'll bash his bloody brains out! I'll… I'll… smash up his camera! I'll… I'll… set his house on fire!' Poor Yash had become incoherent.

In the next room, his mother raised her eyebrows and sighed. Was that another of Yash's friendships biting the dust? She got up and went to the door.

'Yash, calm down will you!' she said popping her head around the door and looking at him disapprovingly. He was bright scarlet in the face and was banging the telephone table with his fist making the pens dance. 'What's the matter? Keep your voice down! And whatever it is, there's no need to shout and be rude!'

Yash looked up and breathed heavily. Okay, cool it, cool down, you have to calm down and play this out carefully or she'll suspect something. Somehow, anyhow he'd have to go back to Shanbagh. If that creep… No question, he'd have to go back! But how? By bus… He'd seen where the bus stop was. He looked up at his mother and smiled.

'Sorry mom! It's okay! I just got a little excited talking to Maya. Imagine she went into the sea and picked the baby out of it!'

'Yes, she was very brave wasn't she? It's good to know someone like that!' She smiled, so the little friendship had not ended.

Yash stomped off into his room and looked around. Okay, so he could pack some stuff into his knapsack, sneak out at night and catch a bus to Shanbagh. He hadn't a clue as to which bus went there, but he knew where the bus stand was, and people there would know. He had just begun stuffing things into his knapsack when the door opened and his mother popped her head around it again.

'I forgot to tell you, Yash. It's your birthday day after tomorrow and Papa and I have planned a special surprise for you…'

Too bad! By day after tomorrow he'd be back at the resort bashing Hari's brains out and setting the place on fire.

'Thanks,' he said and didn't even probe what kind of surprise.

She'd noticed the open knapsack and cupboard. 'I thought you'd finished unpacking,' she remarked.

'I lost one of my admirals,' he replied. 'And was searching for him.'

'Aren't you going to ask me what kind of treat?' his mother asked surprised, coming into the room and sitting on his bed. Oh God, now she'll be here for the next half an hour. 'Normally you pester us to exhaustion.'

'Okay, so what's the great surprise?'

'We're thinking of going back to Shanbagh Resort tomorrow, so you can celebrate your birthday there. With your friend – she's the only friend you've made on this trip after all…'

He looked up and stared at her incredulously. 'We're going back… to the resort?' he whispered. His mother smiled and nodded, and then looked at him in concern.

'Yash, are you all right?'

'I'm fine, Mom, fine. And thanks!'

'So start packing,' his mother added briskly and walked out of the room.

'You know,' she said to her husband, smiling. 'We've got one lovesick little Romeo back there. The little guy had tears in his eyes when I told him that we're going back to the resort. He's really fallen for that girl!'

Mr Ahuja shook his head. 'I can understand his having a crush on the girl. What I can't is what she sees in the rascal!'

'If anything,' Mrs Ahuja said softly. 'I fear little Yash might have to find out the hard way!'

Of course she couldn't have been more wrong.

11

The waiting was the worst. It always was. That morning, Hari had rung her up.

'I can't come down to the Rock this morning,' he told her as if he were disappointing her hugely, 'Papa's left me in charge here.' He paused, 'But tonight's on definitely!' She could hear him suck in his spittle. He went on, 'Low tide is at 10.45 p.m., so that gives us pretty much the whole night on the Rock. We can get back at around 7 or 7.30 in the morning as the tide begins to recede again. And if anyone sees us then, they'll just assume that we'd gone for an early morning walk on the beach.' He breathed heavily, significantly, 'I hope you're looking forward to this Maya, as much as I am. You should be! Ah, yes, and wear a dark T-shirt and shorts over your swimsuit!' Conspiratorial now. 'Bye, be seeing you!'

She put down the receiver and stared dully out at the sea. Perhaps she could break an arm or a leg or something, she'd be out of his clutches forever then. But she knew how vindictive he could be; he'd release the disc just to spite her. Maybe she should do what Yash had suggested, sneak into his room and destroy his computer and camera and discs and set it all on fire. But he'd probably be viewing that disc every five minutes and gloating… that option was not very feasible either. And what would happen afterwards, she wondered. He'd probably want her there on the following night and the night after that, certainly as long as his parents and Sherry were out, and probably even afterwards. Something would give, it would have to, she couldn't continue like this for much longer.

To distract herself as much as possible, she leafed through her beautiful encyclopedia of shells, trying to identify some of the specimens in her biscuit tin.

'Right!' she said, picking out a glossy beauty with an intricate and delicate orange weave all over it. 'You look like a Ming vase, let's see what you were!' She leafed through the book and gave a cry, 'Ah, got you, here you are!' A few minutes later she sat back and pushed the hair from her face, astonished. 'Wow! Will you look at that! So beautiful and so deadly Ms *Conus textile*! The gorgeous shell, she read, was one of several famous for their lethal neurotoxic venom. It was hard to imagine this beautiful creature once skulked about at the bottom of the sea, sniffing its victims out and then harpooned them with a venomous barb. How Yash would have loved it! She gave a small smile, 'Ah if only you had been alive, I know just the person you could have nailed!' And sat back and murmured:

A mollusk from the family Conus
Could have easily taken on the onus
Of harpooning Hari the creep
Crawling about in the deep
And given me a humongous bonus!

She hardly ate anything for dinner that night, and sat blankly in front of the TV waiting for the dreadful hour. Why, why, why had she been such a coward and fool and not set right the record when she had had the chance? All she had had to do was to take that mike and tell the world what had really happened. And that she was terribly sorry and thankful that some guardian angel of the sea had rescued little Asha, even as she had turned her back on her. People would have looked up to her for owning up. Instead like a crook she had claimed, and basked in, the glory of something she had not done. That other little crook, Yash, of course had seen it in a different light entirely and that's what she loved about him so much. She smiled wanly; well she had pulled one off on the media, though she wished it hadn't had to be Arvind Uncle and Smita who were involved.

It was a beautiful night. The moon had risen at about ten, butter yellow and so enormous you could see the craters clearly. Far away the sea glimmered faintly, sighing as the tide pulled out. At around eleven, she heard the gate squeak and looked up startled. Hari was creeping up the path, glancing furtively this way and that like a thief. Maybe… maybe she should whack him over the head with something and claim that she had thought he had been an intruder (which was the truth) but the consequences of that would be disastrous for her.

He spotted her and grinned.

'Ready and waiting? Great!'

He was wearing his black jeans and T-shirt again – to be invisible in the dark. He came up next to her. 'This is like eloping,' he whispered wetly, and added. 'Only we can elope over and over again as long as you're here!' He'd brought his waterproof camera bag along she noted with a sinking heart. 'Come on, Maya, let's go!'

She dithered as long as she could and then stepped out with him. He grabbed her hand before she could protest or snatch it back, and led her with exaggerated caution down the rocky steps and on to the beach.

'We'll run from rock to rock,' he whispered. 'Once we're in the causeway we'll be safe, we can creep along the rocky sides.' It was almost midnight by the time they got to Razor Rock 3; he had taken his time en route, pausing at rock pools and glancing at her, enjoying her discomfiture.

'Just look at the size of those crabs!' he said, as if he had crabs on his mind. 'They would be absolutely delicious. Come on, Maya I thought we'd go to the little cove first! I want to try out some shots by moonlight!'

By now the moon was riding high and silver and the little cove was beautiful, the sand glimmering beneath the silvered waters, the rocks inky craggy silhouettes, the wavelets silver-tipped. Poor Maya saw nothing of this, but Hari was working himself up into a high state of excitement. He paced up and down the little silver beach, frowning and making frames with his hands as if deciding shots and angles. She sat down on a rock and stared out, the wind gently tugging her hair. Hari had stripped down to his trunks and his body glimmered sickly pale in the moonlight.

'Okay,' he said. 'Take off your shorts and T-shirt… Not the swimsuit – just yet.'

It was a nightmare beyond belief. He played his hideous camera over every inch of her body, silvered and gleaming by the moonlight and sea. Occasionally he would pause, breathing hard, and take a stroll to control himself. She did what he said like a zombie. This was not happening to her, this was happening to something else. So far he hadn't really laid his hands on her, but that would come, she had no doubts about that. He was finding it increasingly difficult to stop his panting every time he pointed his camera at her.

'Okay,' he said at last, patting it. 'I think I've got all I need for the moment. You can put your swimsuit back on!' He reached out for her hand. 'Come on Maya, I want to take you somewhere very special now!' So this was it! He led her to the end of the cove and clambered over some rocks.

'Careful!' he said, tugging at her so that she half-fell on him and he could squeeze a breast. 'Right,' he said, putting away his camera in its waterproof bag and holding it up; 'now just follow me!'

And stepped into the channel that separated Razor Rock 3 from Little Rock.

Maya and Yash had never got down to exploring this part of the Rock as they had intended to, and she paused now and looked around. Some thirty feet across the channel, Little Rock rose, with a retinue of smaller rocks arranged in front of it, the tallest of these shaped like an obelisk. To the west, and seawards, a ring of high rocks stood guard, defiantly keeping the sea from rushing into the channel directly. She could hear the waves crash over them, spilling water into the channel and tossing the spray high. But the sea was insidious and would have its way – waves circled round the far side of Little Rock and swirled back in over a relatively shallower shelf of rocks. Thus two opposing movements of water, met in this turbulent channel, tossing up defiant little whiteheads now silver-tipped with moonlight. It seemed that the tide had already started coming in again, for the water swirled and swished busily in the channel. 'Oops!' Hari called about halfway across, balancing himself, now about waist deep. 'The tide's coming in quite fast! Come on Maya!' He laughed and pointed up Little Rock at the alcove. 'That's where we're going to find sanctuary tonight!'

She stared at the swirling silvered waters, shivering slightly. No she wouldn't be out of her depth – but to be 'stranded' with him on that rock… for the rest of the night… He had reached the base of Little Rock and was stepping carefully around the rocks littered in front of it. A wave swirled in, and buffeted him, and he laughed. 'Come on,' he called. 'What are you waiting for? Do you want to be on the news tomorrow? Plus I have all this footage I can put on the net! Would you like the whole world to see that?'

Footage of her naked in the moonlit sea.

She choked back a sob and put a foot into the water and began wading in carefully.

Another wave came sweeping in, and she clutched at a rock for balance; don't panic, don't panic, don't panic, it's only a little over knee deep, what's your problem, Maya. He was balancing on the rocks at the other end, looking at her and wondering if he ought to get his camera out and tell her to take off her swimsuit again.

So engrossed that he didn't hear or notice the soft heavy clunk, as a wave shifted a badly balanced rock and deposited it gently over his foot, hardly touching it, but like a trap closing gently. He felt no pain, but when he tried to shift his position he found he couldn't move. He was caught fast at the ankle, and could not move the foot in any direction. For a moment he was surprised, no lateral movement, so how about back and forth then? No? No! It seemed like his foot had been buried in cement.

'Maya!' he called, 'come on! Hurry up. I think my foot's stuck! Help me free it!'

He smiled. God was great! It would give him another good chance to clutch and grope her closely – a nice prelude to things to come. The foot would come free eventually… But maybe, maybe it would be better if he could free it himself after all, and *pretend* it was stuck…

Another powerful swell rocked him. It was a full moon night and the spring tide was running strong. Maya looked at him with loathing. 'It's just another cheap trick to feel me up,' she thought. As though he's not going to get enough of that once she was in that alcove with him. He was standing upright now, holding the obelisk shaped rock rearing up beside him for balance.

'Maya! Come on!' He slung his camera bag around his neck (it was guaranteed waterproof so he wasn't too worried about it) and bent down and felt around with his hands. The rock on his foot had settled itself firmly and did not budge. He tried once again, and nearly gave himself a hernia, but the rock didn't give an inch. He stood up again and tried pulling his leg out but it did not budge. Halfway across herself, and balancing gamely against the waves slapping against her thighs, Maya gave a squawk of fright as a ruffian wave nearly lifted her off her feet. She backed away and was soon perched at the edge of Rock 3 again. So he was pretending he was stuck… well two could play the same game and let's see how he liked that.

Hari!' she called tremulously. 'I can't come now. The water's getting higher! You know how afraid I am of it. You filmed me remember with Asha… turning back. You have it on disc! All the proof you need!'

'Maya, stop it!' he shouted, and struggled suddenly like a buffalo hit by a cattle prod. The damn foot was still held fast and would not come free, and the first tentacles of fear were wrapping themselves around him. Maya stiffened: There had been a raucous note in Hari's voice… was that panic? She could see him struggling now, and grimacing. Ah, so maybe he was stuck after all – it served him right if he was. But… but… the tide was coming in swiftly now, ironically the water sweeping in from the leeward side. It was rising quickly, inexorably, swallowing rocks by the moment. Another wave had smacked him hard and the water was now swirling about his chest. And Maya felt a cold, cold fear clutch her heart like an ice tong and squeeze it. No! Oh God, this was not happening. Not again! No!

'Maya!' there was sheer panic in Hari's screech as he too realized what would very shortly happen if he did not get his foot free. He was clinging to the obelisk shaped rock with both arms now, and with horror had noticed the high water mark on it – four feet above his head. 'Please, help me out of here!'

She took a deep breath and lowered herself into the swirling waters. And immediately was nearly rocked off her feet and withdrew quickly. 'I can't do it! I can't do it! I just can't!' she screamed. And whimpered, 'I'm sorry!' She crouched on her rock, her hands in front of her face.

'Maya, I'm sorry! I'm sorry! I'll destroy all the discs. I'm sorry for everything. Please, please get me out of here!' He was blubbering now. 'See I mean it!' Desperately he unslung his camera bag and flung it at the rocks, and even above the tumult of the waves, Maya heard it crunch and smash before it dropped and sank. He was howling now, trying desperately to free his foot.

Maya clutched her ears, and shut her eyes and breathed deeply.

'I hate you God!' she screamed suddenly, driven beyond endurance. 'Damn you, damn you, damn you! You're no God! No God would do this to me twice! You're a devil God! A devil! You're worse than Hari! See how you like this now! Enjoy yourself you sadistic twisted pervert!' She glanced across at Hari. The waves were lunging and attacking him like wolves now splashing straight into his face. It wouldn't be long before he went under. For a second she wondered whether she ought to run back and fetch help – but by now the causeway would be awash – and by the time help arrived Hari would be as good as five fathoms under.

'Maya… please! I'm begging you! I'm sorry!' He was holding out one arm towards her clutching the rock with the other so he wouldn't be smashed into them by the waves. Only the obelisk shaped rock stood clear, the others had already gone under.

Okay, okay so this was not the sea, right? It was just a large swimming pool in which someone had started up a wave-making machine. She swam well in pools, so what was the problem? And it was just ten or fifteen metres across. It was now or never.

She closed her eyes and cleaved into the water cleanly. With strong desperate strokes she swam towards the blubbering hulk clinging to the rock.

He clutched out at her desperately, as she trod water near him, astonished that she had made it and balancing herself automatically against the buffeting, not even realizing that she was out of her depth, just about, but still. 'Don't touch me!' she screamed. 'Keep your filthy paws off me!'

'Just… just get me out…' he bawled, and she dared not look at his nose. 'My foot is caught under a rock!'

She held on to the rock for support, then clutched her nose shut and sank under. The silvered waters turned pitch black almost immediately, but she could just make out the unhealthy glimmer of his legs. He nearly kicked her in the face with his free leg, and she hit it away from her as hard as she could. The fool had put his leg in a narrow cleft between two rocks, and the third, the wobbly but heavy one had just rolled over it and settled comfortably on top of it like a lid. If she could get it off, the foot would slip free. Gasping she surfaced, clutching at the rocks again, and noticing that the waters had now risen up to his chin and were slopping into his mouth. He was keeping his face turned upwards, sheer terror in his eyes, gibbering with fear.

'Don't let me drown!' he blubbered. 'Don't let me drown! I don't want to drown. I don't want to die! No… please!'

'I'm going down again!' she screamed, little realizing that she was now well out of her depth too, as the water level rose. 'There's a rock on top of your foot! Keep your other leg still!'

She dipped under again feeling around with her hands. She found the rock and heaved it with all her might, but couldn't budge it an inch. Okay, so dig beneath it. With enough space underneath maybe he could slip out his foot somehow. She reached down low, feeling with her fingers. But no, there was solid rock at the bottom. No way to dig that out. She shot back up, her breath coming in great whooping gasps. The waves were washing over his face and he was stretching himself to the maximum to keep his nose above them. Not much time now. Down she went again, feeling the water tug and buffet her; she was lucky that because of the great ring of rocks between Rock 3 and Little Rock that blocked the direct access of the sea, no deadly current could be created that could whisk her out to sea. There was pushing and shoving and buffeting yes, turbulence, like people getting on and off a bus simultaneously, but no single powerful force like the hand of the devil in her back. She felt around the rocky bottom with her hands, ignoring the creatures that scuttled away from them and discovered another big rock just adjacent to the ones that held his ankle from the sides. It seemed firmly embedded. She crouched down next to it, leaning her back and bottom against it, both hands on what was now the seabed. Bracing herself thus, she placed her strong runner's legs against the rock that had trapped Hari's foot. And pushed with all her strength. At first nothing and she felt as if her lungs would burst. She felt the sea buffet her in the back repeatedly and in quick succession, lurching her forwards; shoving her in the back strongly now. (As Yash might have put it, 'you had a tailwind!') She waited... come on, come on, come on, just once more! She couldn't hold her breath much longer. She got the timing right at her second attempt and gave another mighty heave a second after the wave shoved her in her back. The rock jammed against her feet, rocked and shifted under the combined force of her legs and the wave and she shoved again before it could settle back. And then she shot up again, and bobbed up like a cork almost even before she felt it shift and roll away. She burst to the surface in a paroxysm of coughing and gasping.

'See if you can move your foot!' she screamed at Hari, 'I think I felt the rock wobble!' He was blubbering and gasping, his head lolling from side to side. She snatched at his hair and yanked his head right back so he faced the sky and the coin-bright moon. He breathed in great whooping gasps and coughed gouts of water out. 'Try lifting your foot now!' she screamed and slapped him hard across the face. 'I think the rock came off it!'

There was such an expression of incredulousness on his face when he realized that this was the case she wanted to laugh. Spluttering and coughing, he trod water and then made desperately for Little Rock. She turned fearlessly now towards Rock 3 and the cove, but realized that the tide had claimed them; even access to Rock 3 now was not possible. And suddenly she realized that she had been way out of her depth in these tumultuous waters and really it was no big deal. Exultantly she swam up and down the channel, 'it's like riding a bicycle for the first time,' she thought as she did her victory laps. But soon there was nothing for it but to clamber after Hari up the rocks arranged so conveniently into steps and into the alcove he had meant to take her in the first place.

The moon poured into the little space, luminescent and silver. Hari who had crawled up like a fat white twitching maggot sat propped up, shaking and sobbing loudly, between spasms of coughing and spluttering and retching. He stared at her amazed as she swam back and forth, relishing every moment of it; had she finally gone crazy? At last Maya hoisted herself into the alcove and looked around warily. Hari was still gulping back great sobs and sniveling.

'Shut up will you Hari!' she snapped tiredly getting her hair out of her face. 'Stop blubbering and wipe your nose for God's sake!' He looked at her out of bloodshot eyes and she stared back at him levelly. 'If you so much as move an inch towards me, I'm going to throw you off this place!' she said. 'I've just about had it with you, Hari! You and your filthy pawing and everything!'

'You… you… saved… You're an angel…'

'And don't think I did this for you! I did it for Asha! You see I don't give a shit anymore about you or your discs. Go peddle them where you want – do what you like with them. I don't care! I don't need to care anymore! I'm not scared of you or… or anything! You're nothing but a filthy, cowardly pervert and have always been one.'

She settled herself at the other side of the little alcove, and closed her eyes. Somewhere inside her something had begun to glow, warming her wondrously. I did it! I did it! I dived into the sea – in the dark too – well out of my depth and swam, she thought exultantly. And had even ducked underwater so many times to free this howling ape. If only… if only she had summoned the courage to do that with little Asha… She glanced at the boiling sea beneath and smiled, 'I could leap into that and swim all the way to Africa now!' she thought exultantly. 'With Yash on my back!' And now, strangely nothing seemed to matter too much; not the fact that she would not appear for her boards this year, or that Arunda and his assholes thought she was gaunt and broody, or that Jay outshone her a hundred to one in whatever he did, or that her mother kept haranguing her for every little thing. Never again would those things eat her insidiously inside out like the larva of some diabolical wasp in some poor insect. Ah, and then there was Yash! She paused, well she didn't quite know, wasn't quite sure how she would deal with Yash. Had he just been a helpless victim of her own inadequacies, someone who could not run when she engulfed him in her arms? Would she feel, did she feel about him now as she had done earlier? She shrugged and smiled… Yash was in a class by himself! Always had been! He was Yash and there was no other way she could think about him. The ape was staring at her, still half terrified, tremors shaking him from time to time.

'Maya, I swear… I swear I will destroy that disc! In front of you! God promise!' He clutched his ears and would have touched her feet had she not snatched them back.

'Don't you ever dare touch me again! I told you, I'll push you over. And if you… if you ever mention to anyone what happened here tonight…I'll tell them what you'd been doing to me all these days. And don't think they won't believe me. Smita and Maria have already suspected…'

'I promise! I promise on my mother, on my father, on Sherry…' He was blubbering again.

'Don't bring poor Sherry into this, and shut up will you,' she said tiredly. 'I'm sick of you!' She drew up her knees and rested her chin on them, her arms wrapped around her legs. It was going to be a long night ahead but she could sit it out calmly. Eventually Hari's head dropped to his chest and he nodded off, still whimpering fitfully from time to time. Maya stared out of the alcove, at the moonlit seascape and knew there would be no more black limericks tormenting her again.

It was well after midnight that same night that the Ahujas drove into Shanbagh Resort again tired after a long and harassing journey. They had meant to get in much earlier, but an accident on the ghat road had delayed them considerably. In the back Yash was asleep. Or seemed to be. They were shown their rooms and sleepily he bade his parents' goodnight.

Ten minutes after the light under his parents' room door went off, Yash slipped out into the dark corridor outside. With ease born of long practice, he slunk out of the lobby and into the garden. He made a beeline for the cottage where Maya and her mother had been staying, keeping well in the shadows. He flitted up into the veranda and then peered in through the window of what he knew was her bedroom, flashing his small torch in short bursts. The curtains were drawn and he couldn't see much. He tried the door and to his joy it opened under his hand. Poor Maya had been too distraught to shut it properly when she had left with Hari earlier that night. But there was no one in the house.

So where was Maya?

At the lout's villa then? Had he taken her there? She had said something about the rocks, but it might be better if he checked the villa out first just in case. No point going all the way out to the rocks to find they were back here all the time.

It was trickier sneaking into the villa, but as the boss was away the guards were sprawled in the verandas on comfortable loungers, fast asleep. A French window on the first floor had been left open, and it took Yash just a few minutes to shin up the rough laterite wall and slip inside. Breathing deeply, he flashed his torch around… Had to be a girl's room, what with that overloaded dressing table and battalions of bottles – that Sherry female obviously. He went into the corridor and slipped into an adjoining bedroom.

Hari's room. But no Hari and no Maya. So, so maybe he had dragged her off to the Rock after all. His gaze fell on Hari's computer, its monitor winking and he paused. He could never resist computers. Quietly he went over and booted it. His eyes widened and he whistled under his breath as he scanned the files, and then started rummaging in the drawers in the desk. It was close to three in the morning when Yash got up shocked by the time he had spent here and even more shocked by what he had discovered. But heck, he'd abandoned poor Maya to her fate with that gorilla. If that bastard had taken her to the Rock while he had been diddling on the computer…. What an ass he had been. He shinned down the wall and charged out onto the deserted beach.

And drew up defeated. The tide was swishing in and already the causeway between Rock 2 and Rock 3 was awash. He ran up to Rock 2 and clambered up on to it. If they were there, they would have to walk past him…

It was a long stakeout for the impatient boy and stared as he did towards Rock 3, he saw no movement on it or any flash of light. Eventually he dropped off, and awoke with a start with the sun bright in his eyes. It was just about seven according to his canary-yellow wristwatch. The causeway, he saw was still under water, though the level was falling fast. At about seven twenty, he realized that the tide, in retreat now, had given back possession of the causeway to Rock 3. Time to get going, boy, he said and then stopped and stared.

A figure was walking–staggering, limping, dragging itself–down the causeway from near Rock 3, towards where he was. Yash waited his jaw dropping further as the figure drew close. It was the lout cousin. But he looked as if he had been in a fight with some terrible sea demon. His hands and arms and shoulders were crisscrossed with scratches and cuts and bruises. His eyes were red-rimmed and watering. His nose was running (but wasn't it always) with some horrible green stuff. He was barefoot. One ankle appeared swollen and badly bruised. He dragged himself slowly past the astonished little boy, saying nothing. As he passed, he gave a muffled sob and snuffled disgustingly. Yash rolled his eyes.

And so where was Maya? Had this half-dead apparition drowned her?

He gazed back towards Rock 3, and a slow grin broke out. There she was, walking towards him, and there was something in the way she walked that Yash had never seen before. Like she was walking but not touching the ground. She was in her swimsuit and barefoot. For a second his face darkened… but then he remembered the condition of the lout. He dropped off the rock and onto the causeway.

'Halt!' he cried. 'Who passes this way?'

She stopped and looked at him.

'The Siren Queen of the deep!' she said tiredly, trying hard to hold back her smile and tears.

'And that?' he jerked a thumb at the retreating figure of the lout.

'An evil demon she battled with and bested.'

'Maya, what did you do to him?'

'Come on, let me tell you!'

For a second she hesitated. Could she bear it if he touched her? Would she flinch like she had with Hari? She looked at his eager beaming face and shrugged. How could she? He was Yash.

She took his hand and led him back to Rock 3.

He was incredulous, awestruck, wonderstruck, thunderstruck and most of all horrorstruck. 'You mean… you mean after all he did to you, you *saved* him? You jumped into those turbulent storm-tossed waters and pulled him out? I would have watched him drown and clapped!'

'I think I saved myself too, Yash. Forever! From everyone! I've never felt like this before!'

'That too, but still…' He paused to think, and his eyes lit up. 'Well, I've saved you too Maya,' he said proudly. 'All night I spent saving you!'

'What are you talking about?'

'These!' he said taking out an album of CDs from his pocket. He picked one out. 'This one, is the rescue one – look he even called it 'The Rescue of Asha by Maya…' He bent it over and snapped it.

'And the others?'

'I couldn't check them all so I just took them, he said simply. He pulled out another, 'But this one – his father might like to see what his crack sting journalist son has been up to in the hotel bathrooms!'

'Oh, God no!'

'And I don't think he'll be able to use his computer ever again!' Yash said with some satisfaction. 'In fact I'm pretty sure he won't!'

(Andsoonafterhehadstaggeredhomeandswitchedonhiscomputer, Hari knew there was something terribly wrong with it. And amidst rising panic discovered his top secret CDs – including the Maya rescue one – missing.)

And now, back on the ledge on Razor Rock 3 they settled down and Yash glanced at her. Something seemed to be bothering him.

'Maya,' he began innocently, 'you know the last time we were here?'

'Yes'.

'Did it really happen? I mean… I mean I keep thinking about it… I can't believe it. Did it happen or was I dreaming…'

'Yes,' she said glancing at him, raising a quizzical eyebrow. Just what was he getting at now? 'Of course it did.'

'You sure?'

'Yash, what are you up to? Of course I'm sure!'

He got up, his familiar cheeky grin plastered all over his face and stepped forwards.

'Er...,' he said, frowning, 'I think I've forgotten. Will you show me again, please?'

Epilogue

Neither Hari nor Maya nor Yash ever mentioned the events that took place at the Rocks on that moonlit night when the spring tide ran strong, to anyone. Hari crawled home that morning, bathed himself with Betadine and Mercurochrome and emerged looking like the walking wounded from the Somme. He said he'd fallen badly into a rock pool while filming crabs and had dropped his precious camcorder into the sea in the accident. Subsequently, he lost all interest in crusading sting-type journalism and has announced to his alarmed parents that he wants to shave his head and 'renounce the world' and move to an ashram in Bihar. He's taken his full name Harishchand. It can only be hoped that the future Swami Harishchand is able to keep his hands to himself and his nose clean.

Sherry returned from Bombay to find a very changed brother, but simply thought that he had been royally dumped by Neha (who had a reputation for this kind of thing) and would eventually recover. She was of course, hugely thrilled with Maya and Yash, 'you two are really thick as thieves!' she squealed, hugging them both (to Yash's deep mortification).

Maya and Yash had a wonderful time for the rest of that summer. They fought many more epic sea battles in the cove, but are more careful about the happy aftermaths of those battles. Maya did manage to sweet talk her uncle into organizing scuba diving and snorkelling classes for his guests at the resort, and of course was the first to enroll. Her interest in shells and mollusks developed considerably and she told Yash, 'This is something I really don't mind studying about all day! They're just so fascinating. So beautiful and so deadly! Gorgeous and yet able to inflict so much pain!' And Yash, of course, grinned and advised her in the manner of the best crooks, 'Yeah, you'd better study them well. Especially about those venomous ones – you never know when you meet another Hari!' But she watched, with equal fascination as he sat down and painstakingly and lovingly repaired, painted and varnished his battered warships after every major battle. 'You're going to join the Navy, or become a crafstman,' she predicted. 'I can bet on that!'

For a while she debated whether she should tell Smita the truth about what happened with Asha. In the end she decided not to, 'Some things are better left unsaid!' she told Yash, who thought she was mad to even think of the idea. It still bothers her from time to time, even though she does think that she's paid her debt through her rescue of Hari. She still delights Yash with her 'spontaneous limericking' and he's given her a whole list of villains from his past he wants 'limericked' ('so I can e-mail them!' he said gleefully). Much to his (and Maya's) joy, his parents did decide to set down roots after all – in New Delhi – settling down in a house not far from where Maya lives. And at the time of writing at least, it seems highly unlikely that (as Smita had told her) what they have together will ever fade away and become just a warm and sweet memory.